HAUNTED DESIGN

Also by Peter H. Green

BIOGRAPHY

Ben's War with the U. S Marines
Radio: One Woman's Family In War and Pieces
(With Alice H. Green}
Becoming an Architect: *My Voyage of Discovery*

PATRICK MACKENNA MYSTERY

Chicago's Designs
Fatal Designs
Crimes of Design

HAUNTED HEARTS

When architect Patrick MacKenna and his pregnant wife Kitty leave their lakefront apartment in search of a home for their growing family, their journey leads them to a crumbling Victorian Gothic mansion. It's perfect for showcasing Patrick's work and impressing clients—if they can bring it back to life. Despite warnings from his business partner and a grisly discovery in the basement, Patrick remains committed to restoring the estate. But his ex-fiancé—his mob client's daughter—has a secret that can unravel everything, and a detective advises them to walk away, Patrick and Kitty must decide if their house restoration is worth the cost, danger, and unknown intruders they must fight to succeed.

CHET'S DILEMMA

Chet now understood his critical role in the process. Until this moment he had felt sufficiently briefed for the inspection tour. But in the cold rain at this moment, the height, extent, and time-worn aspect of the property chilled him to the bone. This imposing Victorian pile dwarfed the little group assembled for the visit. He felt small and helpless, inadequate, his hopes for confronting and subduing this this proud behemoth dashed. He suspected that a two-story rose-covered cottage with a nice yard in in the near suburbs might still be closer to Kitty's hopes for a family home.

PRAISE FOR CHICAGO'S DESIGNS

Peter Green's two central themes, Architecture and Chicago, are linked with magic. His descriptions of Chicago architecture, the city of big shoulders and mob activity are strikingly similar to my own observations as a young architect in Chicago. Green's insights into architectural practice are spot-on. Rich, exciting, fun and a real page turner, this is the best mystery of architecture and Chicago since The Devil in the White City. –Robert O. Little, Former President, Ittner Architects

When a womanizing young architect meets a mobster with a multi-million dollar casino project and a beautiful daughter, what could go wrong? For Patrick MacKenna, "Chicago Joe's" plan to go legit is the career break he's been looking for, and dating the mobster's daughter is icing on the cake. Then Patrick finds himself attracted to a lovely barmaid fresh from Ireland, jeopardizing the deal and maybe even his life. With a murder investigation already linked to the casino property, Patrick turns amateur sleuth to find out who's responsible. This intriguing glimpse into Patrick's early years brings together fast-moving action, architecture and romance in a satisfying prequel to the Patrick MacKenna mystery/thriller series. –T.W. Fendley, Author of the Zero Time Chronicles

Chicago's Designs is…riveting…a gripping whodunit about murder, the mob, sex and love. A terrific read! —David Margolis, Author of *The Misadventures of Buddy Jones*

I am an architect and a serious mystery reader. So Mr. Green checked off two important boxes right away…kept it up and educated and entertained me the rest of the way. —Randall B. Miltenberger, AIA , Miltenberger Architects, Inc.

Green has an uncanny ability to describe scenes, develop characters, and create suspense   —Nathan Manhart, Member, St. Louis Writers Guild

HAUNTED DESIGN

A Patrick MacKenna Mystery

By

PETER H. GREEN

Greenskills Press

St. Louis

Haunted Design, A Patrick MacKenna Mystery
By Peter H. Green

Publisher: Greenskills Press, St. Louis, MO
Copyright ©2025 by Peter H. Green

Cover Design ©2025 by Peter H. Green
Cover illustration: Montage of 2nd Empire Victorian Gothic houses, compiled, adapted, configured, modified, and rendered by the author from historical sources: HistoricBuildingsct.com. Silas-Webster Robbins House, Second Empire style mansion on Broad Street Green Wethersfield (CT), 1873, and cupola tower from John M. Davies House of 1868 in New Haven. Source: https://historicbuildingsct.com . Used with opt-in consent from website.

Interior Book Design: Greenskills Press

Address comments and inquiries to:
Greenskills Press, Publisher
An imprint of Greenskills Associates, LLC
P. O. Box 11292
St. Louis, MO 63105

First Edition

This is a work of fiction and is produced from the author's imagination. Any resemblance to specific individuals is purely coincidental. People, places, and things mentioned in this novel are used in a fictional manner.

ISBN 13: 978-1-941402-19-1 Trade Paperback
ISBN 13: 978-1-941402-20-7 e-book

Visit us on the web at www.authorpetergreen.com

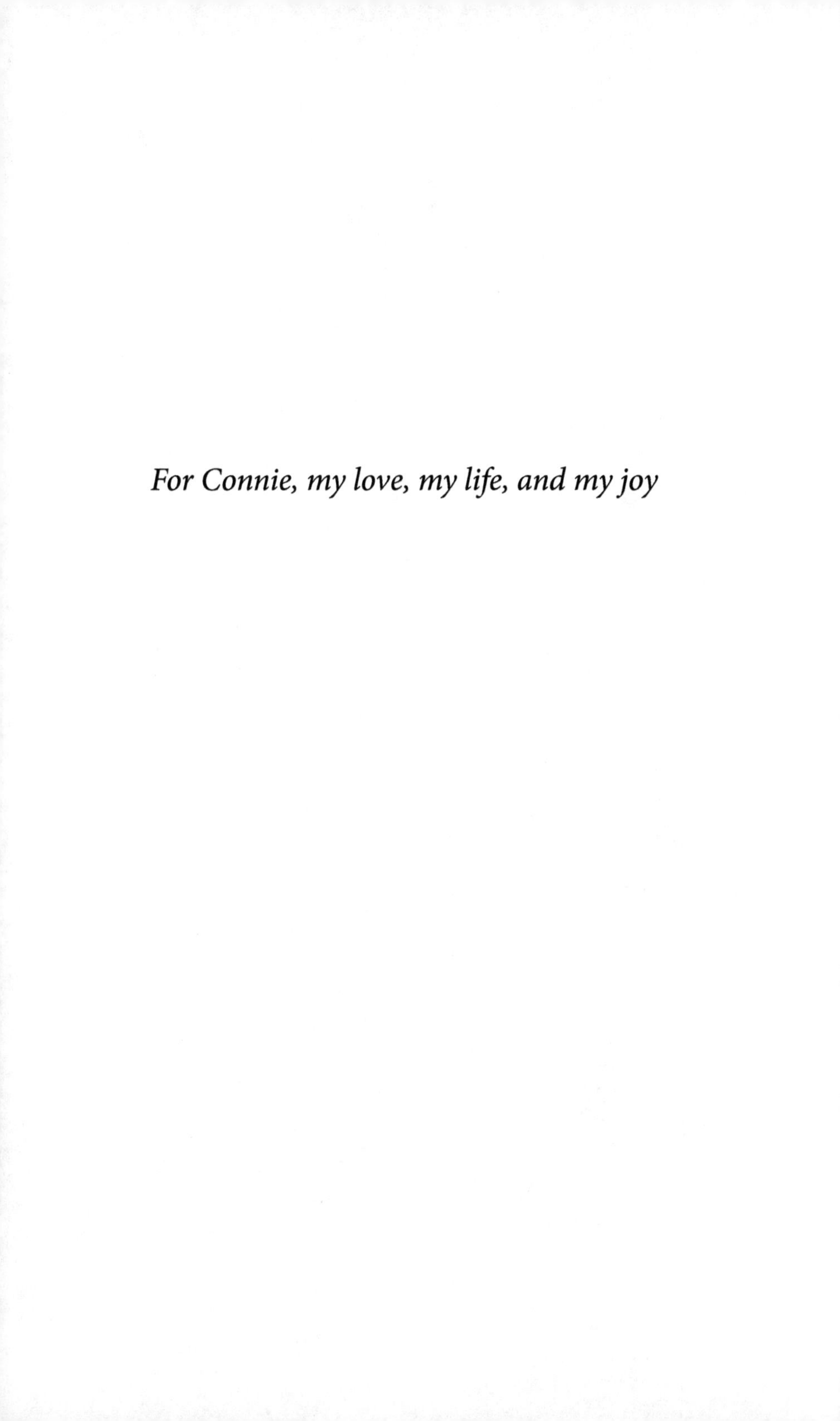

For Connie, my love, my life, and my joy

HAUNTED DESIGN

Part I: Designing Men

Your immigrants here steal and kill till they have the local franchise for sin, and they sell liquor and drugs and women, on license from City Hall. Reformers might call it kickbacks or bribes, but it is, finally, merely a license.

The politicians who oppose them, those who cannot be bribed, if such there be, are currently killed, in time, and one may, perhaps, see it already, the Irish and the Italians, will ask why not become politicians? And they will.

They, as soldiers to one another, will have taught themselves the foremost lessons: study the ground. Then they will not only possess the sin franchise, but every other fungible good, service and permission.

—David Mamet, *Chicago,* 2018

Chapter One

Dark clouds over an angry lake obscured the fiery sun. Patrick never knew what a new Chicago day would bring. But today the prospect from his glass walled Lake Shore Drive apartment did not bode well. The jingle, "Red sky in morning, sailor take warning," drummed in his head. A cool front sliding in from the northwest was bringing in the first taste of a severe oncoming winter. In the bedroom, gloomy morning light barely penetrated the gauzy curtains. Kitty slept peacefully, with her loyal dog Buster under the covers at her side.

He filled the dog's water dish, grabbed a handful of treats, and set them near the bed. He took the rose from a bud vase near the sink, placed it on her pillow, and kissed her forehead.

"M-mm," she whispered, and snuggled deeper into her dream.

Without disturbing them further, he packed his briefcase, donned his mackintosh, and left for the office.

The news that Patrick and his young bride Kitty were having a baby generated even more excitement than had the couple's wedding a year earlier. Their friends and families in Chicago, and especially those back in Ireland, were thrilled and planned a repeat of last year's gala event — an all-expenses-paid celebration to be held at the site of Patrick's latest architectural project: a casino, hotel, and vacation destination. The resort was an hour's drive north of Chicago along the bank of the Rock River. Joseph "Chicago Joe" Bohannon, Patrick's client for the project, and his wife Candy would be delighted to host the visitors and welcome a new member to their growing family.

Patrick MacKenna, an up-and-coming young architect, and the charming, gifted and capable Kitty O'Connor had made an illustrious match — as most seemed to agree. They had met at the MacKenna family's downtown Irish pub, where talented singers and musicians immigrated, to wait tables and perform authentic Irish music for overflowing crowds. The couple shared their cultural heritage, a common interest in design, and a strong mutual attraction but had complementary yet contrasting personalities. He had boundless vision, energy, and optimism; and she, with an independent outlook, a ready wit, and a firm grip on reality, kept his expansive ego within tolerable limits.

Not everyone, however, was delighted with this marriage. Gloria Bohannon, Joe and Candy's daughter, had been Patrick's fiancé. She considered her influence one of the main reasons her father had entrusted this dream project to the young architect. She felt jilted and resentful at this immigrant upstart's sudden appearance on the scene. Kitty had known Patrick for less than a year, while Gloria had known him much longer. She had seen their union as a key part of her plan — not only to run the enterprise Joe Bohannon had created for her as his lifetime legacy, but also to marry Patrick, one of its principal creators.

Patrick and his professional partner Chet Neuzing first met seven years earlier at Holdroyd & Robb, both fresh out of architecture school. They suffered together through apprenticeship, the trials of earning their architectural licenses, and the intricacies of finishing low-paying remodeling projects nobody else would take on. Lucky to team up, they needed each other. Patrick was the visionary, the brains of the outfit. Chet was his right hand — problem solver and confessor in most things, even girl troubles. In the batting order Chet was the clean-up man, justifying, clarifying, and implementing Patrick's designs. It would be hard to say which one was the mentor. Seemingly joined at the hip, they were a smooth functioning team.

On this stormy day Patrick strode into Chet's cube to announce: "We're buying a house!" Because of their close relationship, he was taken by surprise.

"Congratulations, how exciting!" Chet responded.

But the declaration struck fear into his heart. "What does that mean, exactly — we're buying?" he asked.

"Just that," Patrick said. "Kitty and I put a contract in last week, and it was accepted. Will you inspect it with me Saturday?" He mentioned an address on the Northwest side.

"Oh sure, you idiot." He couldn't refuse to help Patrick, but he still felt left out. Where had he been while all this was happening?

When it came to the big idea, the design concept, Chet knew when to shut up. But in practical matters, he needed to offer sound advice. "Heck," he said, "in that neighborhood, it's probably haunted." Patrick took the comment as a wisecrack, but it would hardly deter him, since he had clearly made up his mind.

"What, you believe in that nonsense?"

"Maybe, maybe not," Chet said. "Generally, I reserve judgment about the supernatural. After all, my wife and I are church-going people. But still, you've got to be crazy!"

"I would be crazy to pass this up." Patrick said. "Near downtown, a classic style, a perfect estate for an architect. At a bargain price."

"If you were stuck with it as a bequest from an estate, maybe — but not a place you'd go out and buy. Are you sure the gangsters no longer have a hideout near there?"

"We helped put the worst of them in prison, out of circulation for quite a while. There's been no sign of the others since. Now we can jump on this great opportunity."

"Couldn't you just buy a nice modern house in the suburbs?" Chet protested. The property was in a once fashionable block on the Northwest Side next to an old industrial district. Newlyweds with limited funds, he and Kitty were looking at fixer-uppers. True, sometimes these gracious old buildings looked like bargains. But hidden deterioration and obsolete building systems posed added risks that could blow anyone's budget to bits. He had visions of rotting wood, burnt-out wiring, and leaking pipes. His rehabilitation experience reminded him that renovation of one area makes adjacent rooms look bad.

"By the time you fix it up, you'll spend a lot more."

"You kidding? This is a dream house!"

Reluctant to encourage his folly, Chet resolved at least to inspect and get him untangled from the deal if necessary.

Without question, Patrick was the dreamer of the two — romantic, sure of himself and stubborn as a mule in getting his way. He drove the truck and kept the hammer down. Chet was the navigator, reality checker and mechanic that kept things in good running order. But he'd learned not to form his opinions too fast — to be on the lookout for something in any new project he couldn't yet appreciate. Often, he didn't see beyond the weeds and missed the beautiful forest Patrick saw beyond — options, possibilities, and unexpected outcomes.

While the two architects were different and often disagreed, they were devoted to each other. Patrick was tall, good-looking and an instant hit with the girls. Chet was shorter, fatter and had always been shy with women. He considered himself lucky to find his wife Ellen in college. A mutual friend introduced them with the suspect phrase: "You'll love her, Chet. She has a great personality!" It turned out her friend was right. Although ample-figured and motherly, she was beautiful, unconditionally loving, and willing to believe that even he had a future. Five years ago they had married, bought a three-story duplex and started a family. Patrick remained single, with a short attention span for any woman. Chet had trouble keeping track of his latest girlfriends.

Until Kitty came along. She hit his truck broadside. When she arrived from Ireland with his father's annual troupe of talent to work as wait staff and entertainers at their pub, he couldn't get enough of her. Her red hair, green eyes, trim figure, and the singing voice of a nightingale made a neat little package. Unlike his previous girlfriends, she was witty and quick. She could put him in a corner any time he got too full of himself. He couldn't live without her.

With the recent exciting news of Kitty's pregnancy, Patrick entered a new phase. His outlook, demeanor and nightly routine now focused on the joys and responsibilities of oncoming fatherhood. He began returning home early for dinner every night. Their evenings were devoted to planning for the baby's needs. They knew their high-rise apartment would never do for a growing family — they must find a house. The result: their current decision point.

Over the next two days Chet coaxed Patrick to tell him the story he had missed about their quest for a new house. For an architect with a love for fine old homes, up-to-date efficiency, and functional technology, this challenge had many requirements. He was determined to find a house that would meet his business needs and make a good home for their growing family

Two years ago, through his pursuit of gang criminals who had tried to interfere with his casino resort's progress, he had located them in a hideout in this Northwest Side neighborhood, once the pride of early Chicago industrialists for showplace homes, located near their factories. Now that they had solved the case and seen the perpetrators put away, he believed the coast was clear to look in this neighborhood for an architectural gem which he could show off with pride and adapt to their precise housing needs.

Patrick had long admired a fascinating house a couple of blocks down the street from the former mob hideout. It was one of the finest and tallest of the mansions on the street. Recently, he spotted an ad in the paper for a Victorian on Bond Street. When he recognized the address it made him shiver — whether with excited anticipation or fear of past troubles on the street, he wasn't sure. He called the number, and a pleasant-sounding woman identified herself as the listing agent for the property. The next weekend he and Kitty entered this mysterious house with the obliging realtor Abigail. They were met at the door by one of the owners, a short, soft-spoken young man, Charles Simpson, whom the agent deemed essential for answering prospective buyers' questions about their previous renovation efforts.

After touring the many rooms on three floors Abigail suggested they split up while Patrick inspected technical features of the house in the basement with the owner and she showed the partially renovated kitchen to Kitty.

Simpson took Patrick to the coal bin, which was nearly empty, and demonstrated the Iron Fireman conveyor belt, When the house thermostat called for heat, it delivered more or less of the hard anthracite coal to the firebox.

"I'm familiar with those," Patrick said. "We used to have one in the home where I grew up."

"We're waiting for our winter coal delivery," Simpson said. He pointed out a high window where the coal chute from the truck would pour the coal into the bin. "Now let me show you one of my favorite parts of the house."

He led Patrick through an arched doorway into a long, narrow room with wine racks lining the walls. Many of the bottles were coated with dust. He reached for a higher rack and withdrew a dusty bottle, its labels peeling off and almost invisible. He handed it to Patrick, who recognized it instantly from the raised lettering on the cast glass bottle.

"My God, this is Châteauneuf du Pape, of a very old vintage!" Patrick knew something about good wine and was blown away to hold this rare bottle of French red.

"I know." Simpson sighed. "We'll have to abandon the whole collection. There's no way we can properly transport all this fine wine, much less store it, in any apartments we might rent. But it makes a fine bonus for owning the property." He reached for another bottle from the same rack. Patrick stared in disbelief as Simpson urged him to accept the bottle he was holding and gave him the second bottle as well. "Here, it's our little thank you for your visit today and your interest in our property."

"Why, thank you!" Patrick marveled at his luck and took it as a good omen for their quest. He stashed the bottles in the backpack he carried for his property notebook, and they rejoined Abigail and Kitty on the main floor.

"I believe I could live with this kitchen," Kitty said. "You fellows have done enough modernization to make it usable. A new range and a new dishwasher are all I'd need."

"The same is true for the heating system," Patrick said. "These rooms will clean up very nicely. We'll see about getting the roof repaired, the kitchen improvements you want, and electrical systems updated. Then we can move in right away."

Then, sensing Simpson's despair over leaving, Patrick said, "Are you sorry you have to give up on this house?"

"Yes and no. Because of his only modestly successful writing career, Hensley Wilson, my partner, has had to travel to conferences and accept far-flung, paying assignments to support the expense of his travel. When he was gone for a month or two at a time, it took the fun out of the project. It was more than I wanted to tackle on my own, without his enthusiasm and drive — he's fifteen years younger than me, you know."

"No, I didn't realize —"a perfect time to turn him loose and let him seek a partner closer to his age."

"I understand. It was the kindest and most generous thing you could do for your dear friend."

"I told him on many occasions that eventually I would turn into a fat old relic, who couldn't attract him anymore, nor properly satisfy his needs. But he said he was okay with it. Then he had this Hollywood offer. It will require him to be gone full time for a year or more. The way I saw it, it was, it was the perfect time to turn him loose and seek another partner closer to his age."

"Makes sense."

"Exactly, and it relieved my guilt over limiting his future life."

Patrick had learned something about love, loyalty, and devotion.

Chapter Two

The following Saturday in a raw, cold rain, Chet pulled up to the curb in front of the property. He chuckled. This would make a fitting home for the Gomez and Morticia Addams family. The house was a relic of the 1880s, when prosperous captains of industry competed to have the finest house on this once prestigious street. This industrialist and his architect had conspired to outdo his wealthy neighbors. Chet recognized it as an example of the Second Empire Style, a branch of the Victorian Gothic genre. They had spared no expense in its design and construction, complete with uniquely sculpted roofs in a style first created in the 1870s. When Napoleon III ordered Baron Haussmann to re-plan Paris, he and his architect Francois Mansart lined the new grand boulevards with four- and five-story buildings, featuring "mansard" roofs forming the top-floor walls.

Chet now understood his critical role in the process. Until this moment he had felt sufficiently briefed for the inspection tour. But in the cold rain at this moment, the height, extent, and time-worn aspect of the property chilled him to the bone. This imposing Victorian pile dwarfed the little group assembled for the visit. He felt small and helpless, inadequate, his hopes for confronting and subduing this proud behemoth dashed. He suspected that a two-story rose-covered cottage with a nice yard in the near suburbs might still be closer to Kitty's hopes for a family home.

A slope-roofed porch wrapped around the building's left side and extended across the front. Dormer windows projected like eyebrows from the steep third-floor mansard roofs. On the right the porch ended at a square tower, whose peak featured a cupola with mansard-roofed windows facing in four directions.

As if the grim aspect of this Victorian castle weren't frightening enough, its condition was worse. Even through the misty rain, he noted the dilapidated condition of eaves, balconies, and bay windows and their ornate support brackets. Some of the mansard level's diamond-patterned slates were missing, and the wrought iron cresting that topped off the upper cornice needed repair. Most of the wood trim surfaces craved new paint. Somehow Patrick had seen beyond these shabby surfaces. But replacing deteriorated sections of the fancy trim would require weeks of skilled finish carpenters' attention, and only then could painters scrape off peeling paint and apply new coats to bring out the design's faded beauty.

Patrick's silver Honda rolled to a stop at the curb. Kitty alighted from the passenger seat as if from a coach-and-four, turned and gazed at the Victorian pile, her green eyes taking in the scene, auburn hair aglow in the grey fog. As Chet climbed the porch steps to join the couple and meet the realtor, their dog Buster bounded ahead, straining at the leash Patrick held and wagging his bushy tail to greet him.

The realtor stood waiting on the sagging front porch of the timeworn estate—a grey-haired rail-thin woman with a nervous, twitchy demeanor. She wore a huge, bulky overcoat, likely inherited, whose collar rode up her neck. A monkish cowl further diminished her pinkish-grey face, as if the coat wore her instead of the other way around, and the low-slung hem exposed two slender sticks of support below.

Patrick introduced Chet to Abigail Huntington, the realtor. "This is my colleague, Chet Nuezing. He'll be our building inspector." Her beauty, similarly had faded, but her smile revealed a game approach and a willingness to meet the challenge.

"It rhymes with choosing." Chet said as he extended his hand. He never insisted on the accurate German pronunciation — it helped him fit in.

"Nice to meet you, Mr. Neuzing," she said. I think they've made a wise decision here, don't you?"

He saw no reason to craft an agreeable reply. "We'll see," he said.

"I'll show you its lovely features," she added, still selling. She fiddled with the lockbox, retrieved the key and swung open a massive front door laden with ledges, carved panels and an eye level row of prism-edged glass view lights. Its flat, cylindrical entry knob and brass face plates were embossed with vine tracery, genuine antiques. So far Patrick was batting .500.

Chet stepped across the threshold with trepidation. Despite the current owners' valiant attempts to start renovation, they had largely failed to restore the elaborate interior, which had stood neglected and vacant for an unknown period. The house restoration must have been too much for them. A gilt framed mirror with chipped silvering hung crooked on the left wall of the vestibule. A door on the right wall, she explained, led to the later tower addition. Opposite the front entrance, a glass-paneled inner door opened on a spacious stair well, where a heavy chandelier dangled from the high ceiling, and cobwebs reached it from a ceiling corner. Three flights of stairs wound around the walls to a balcony and a hallway connecting upstairs bedrooms.

In the parlor to the left, original Chippendale side chairs lined the walls. A rolled-arm sofa flanked by matching wing-backed armchairs faced a row of eight-foot-high windows, while worn blue and red Persian carpet anchored the seating group. Chandeliers hanging from chains in the molded plaster ceiling appeared dimly above. Draped with muslin hoods, they loomed like ghosts ready to pounce on any intruders who dared disturb their domain.

Chet's eyes watered and he sneezed five times in a row.

"Sounds like you're allergic to the Victorian atmosphere," Patrick said.

"More likely my dust allergy. You'd have to call in a cleaning crew to scrub down this place and make it livable."

"That would be me, I suppose," Kitty noted. "But it would be worth it. This house has so much soul."

"Let me turn on some lights, while you inspect the upstairs rooms," Abigail said. "I'll lead you as far as the next floor. She seemed to belong to the house, a ghostly guide to its hidden past. She tackled the long stairs. Even the shallow risers were a challenge as she climbed with a wide stride, her knees buckling inward. She must have been in pain. What a cruel fate for her, Chet thought, with an aging frame, to have to earn her living this way.

"The former maid's quarters are in the attic, And you might enjoy the view from the tower," she said. "That's enough stairs for me today. But I'll take the dog." Patrick gladly handed her the leash.

Patrick, Chet, and Kitty followed her up the two-dozen steps, inspected the bedrooms and left Abigail and Buster while the group climbed another flight to the maid's quarters behind the mansard walls of the attic.

"This is a nice little apartment—perfect for our guests." Kitty said. Still higher rose the cupola. Out of shape, Chet puffed and sweated as they ascended again, up the square spiral of the tower stairs. At the top he was forced to squint in the sudden light from dusty windows facing in all four directions. Double-hung frames, their sashes loose, rattled and moaned in the stiff lake gusts ahead of lowering clouds. He shivered, both from the chill and the sheer horror of the place.

The rain had paused enough to reveal a misty distant view. To the north, west and south, acres of residential streets, their predictable rectangles lined with the bare crowns of trembling trees, sprawled for miles across the Chicago prairie. Immediately to the east in the foreground lay the rusting hulks of steel fabrication shops, warehouses, railroad tracks and vacant streets of the disused industrial district. Further east, cut off from this part of the North Side by the murky north branch of the Chicago River, sat many sturdy blocks of residential neighborhoods including his own. Beyond lay the vast inland sea. Winding along the waterfront, Lake Shore Drive peeked out beyond a wall of towers competing along the famous Gold Coast for the highest and best views of its moody waters.

Trying to see this location from Patrick's viewpoint, he wondered, is it so terribly important where you live in this teeming hive? When you consider family safety, helpful neighbors. available schools and resale that rumor about the ghosts and a murder are completely untrue."

"What happened?" Chet wanted to hear more. He was already nervous about the safety of this mostly abandoned residential enclave. On the next block in another Victorian house, Patrick had chased down the perpetrators of a gang assassination and held his client's daughter hostage. It didn't help that the nearby factory district, where the industrialists had long ago made their fortunes, had fallen into neglect.

"Oh, it's a silly story," she continued, "just hearsay, I'm sure. It seems a maid and the butler who worked in this house had secret trysts in the basement. The butler's wife, the family cook, was said to be insanely jealous of the maid. One day she surprised them there and murdered the maid with a butcher's knife."

"That's not so hot," Kitty said. "Surely her spirit is hanging around, haunting the place."

"Kitty, your roots are showing," Patrick said. "That's just old-world superstition."

She once spent an afternoon telling Chet all about the Little People — leprechauns, who can conjure pots of gold at the end of the rainbow and yet are capable of great mischief. They were known to steal babies and brides and cause all kinds of grief for ordinary folk. She went on to describe the various styles of haunting: residual, habitual, and poltergeist. Residual haunting was spiritual energy left in a specific place. The habitual style occurred in various places but was caused by the same spirit. The poltergeist style, literally "noisy spirit" in German, consisted of hidden ghosts, their mysterious footsteps, shifting objects and unexplained sounds.

"I can assure you that those noises the previous occupants heard were from structural shifting in the walls, or perhaps a little animal that got in by mistake." Abigail was determined to dig herself a little deeper in the hole she had created.

"Noises? Oh, no problem, then," Chet said, "except a few invading animals and a little hidden structural failure here and there. So tell me, Ms. Huntington, what gives you the idea there is shifting in the structure?"

"Oh, it's nothing, really." Abigail waved a dismissive hand. "A neighbor down the street told me something she recalled. Some thirty years ago, workmen removed large quantities of brick from the basement in wheelbarrows and loaded it on a truck to haul away. They were creating a game room and had to make space for a pool table."

In the parlor as Chet scribbled these comments on his clipboard. he dropped his pencil. Before he could stoop to pick it up, it rolled to the center hall. He detected a slight slope beneath his feet. Across the hall in the dining room, the pencil rolled the other way to the center. He and Patrick exchanged knowing glances.

"How do we get to the basement?" Chet asked the realtor. She walked to a cellar door and opened it. The two headed toward the steps. Buster yanked the leash free from Abigail and led the way.

They ventured into the musty space illuminated by hanging dim bulbs and peered through the gloomy interior. "Just as I thought," Patrick said. "Do you agree?"

"I knew it — that was a bearing wall they removed. And the only thing holding up the floor is this." Chet pointed to a round metal column supporting an old cast-iron I-beam.

The women had joined us the basement. Kitty remarked, "Imagine all that Victorian charm resting on a single post!" She was falling in love with this ramshackle pile. The two architects knew how to cure the physical problems, but it would not be cheap

"But what about the Little People?" Chet wondered if there were even enough physical remedies to mend the flaws of this house. An appeal to Kitty's fear of forces beyond her control was his last hope to kill the deal and rescue them from this colossal mistake.

"Oh, come on!" Patrick suppressed a grin. "Let's focus on fixing the building defects."

"Ah, not to worry." Kitty said. "Those Wee Folk love mischief and will play tricks on people they don't like. But they're just as likely to be kindred spirits, protecting us loving folks and bringing us good fortune!"

Kitty was rationalizing Chet's objections away.

"It's bad fortune to find this now," Patrick insisted, "but it's a minor structural problem. We could fix it."

"If you go ahead with this deal," Chet added. To his despair, they both had reasons to love the house and wanted to find a way. They had ten days to respond. With the negative findings of his inspection report, their options would be to reject the contract and get their earnest money back or make a counteroffer, enter final price negotiations, and allow the deal to close.

They were about to return upstairs when they heard a howl from the other side of the basement. The small dog's repetitive, ear-piercing bark followed, warning that something was seriously wrong. Then a constant pattern of yips and growls came from the direction of the furnace. Chet found him in a dark corner, assaulting the ancient wooden crib, now filled with coal. As he drew closer, he gagged at an unmistakable odor.

Patrick caught up with him and stared at the scene. The stink of rot was so strong Chet had to tie his handkerchief around his head to breathe. Patrick turned his turtleneck up to cover his nose. He swung open the wooden gate to the coal bin and shined his flashlight on the scene. Buster lunged past him and clamped his jaw on an object mostly buried under the coal pile. Sticking from the heap were a pantleg and a black wing-tipped shoe, and the ankle held firmly in the vise grip of Buster's jaw. When Kitty and Abigail caught up with them, they stood in a tight circle gaping at the spectacle.

Patrick calmed Buster down with soothing phrases and eventually disengaged him from the body. The two of them dragged the dog, straining his leash and constantly turning his head backward, up the steps. They all reassembled in the parlor.

"We've got a legal obligation here," Patrick reminded them. "We have to report this immediately to police and wait for their arrival."

"Oh my God! I've got another showing at two. What am I going to do? I'm just the agent, doing my job. It wasn't I that discovered the body. My day is ruined!" The woman paced in all directions and sputtered, falling apart before their eyes.

"Now Abigail," Patrick said, "get hold of yourself. Call your client and reschedule. Kitty and I were favorably impressed by everything else."

"Oh, thank you," she uttered, reduced to tears.

Patrick put in a call to police headquarters downtown. "Give me O'Malley."

While Patrick was on the phone Kitty led Simpson into the kitchen to clarify what work they had already completed there.

Just his bum luck. O'Malley was there. He sighed. Here we go again. After conversing in hushed tones, Patrick announced: "Detective Sergeant O'Malley's on his way, with the whole team." He turned to Abigail. "What can you tell me about the other seller?"

"Nothing. I'm their confidential agent. If I tell you, I could get in trouble and lose my license."

"You're already in trouble," Patrick said. "It's your listing, and you forgot to check for bodies in the basement. So what can you tell me about the other guy?"

She looked to her right and left and spoke in low tones. "These two young men bought it a several years ago to fix up and make into a showplace. Recently the other owner, Hensley Wilson, got a writing job in Hollywood and moved there. They decided to sell before they got in any deeper.

"The neighboring families were not welcoming," she added. "But the worst part was petty thefts and harassment from the thugs who live up in the next block."

Patrick and Chet knew the place she referred to: the former gang hideout.

"Hmm, they are still there!" he said. "I thought we had cleaned them out."

Chet shook his head and pulled Patrick aside "As if bodies lying around weren't enough, how are you ever going to pay for restoring all this?" The list was long, especially since he wanted to preserve its historical features and restore its original appearance.

"You know how much I love fine, old architecture. And what a place to host our clients! Besides, Kitty loves it. As we get the money, we can do the rehabilitation in phases and spread out the cost over time."

A whole lot of time. Chet listened, but his mind raced. Patrick already had too much on his mind. His dream project — the casino and hotel north of Chicago, was in danger of stalling for a similar reason: lack of funds to begin the next phase. Chet reminded him these were his top priority among the many obstacles this house presented.

"Shifting of the building due to unequal settlement, effects of high winds on the exterior walls, and improper support of floor loads—all are serious issues. It will make the house vulnerable to earthquakes, windstorms, and other outside forces. You'll have to detect and exterminate squirrels, mice or other vermin."

"Think straight, Chet. We're architects, These are all things we understand and can handle."

"What about the crime on the premises?"

"We'll help the police solve it, as we did before."

He'd been helpful to police in solving a downtown murder case. The thought of perpetrators getting away with their scheme haunted him. He would not rest until he had seen justice done. The discovery of a body in this house was just one more obstacle for him to overcome.

Besides, Chet reasoned, there remained other, bigger things to haunt Patrick.

Five years before his own father moved here to open a pub, Patrick's uncle Mike MacKenna arrived in America and worked to become a successful contractor. In his own career, Patrick joined a famous architectural firm, which had designed some of America's first high-rise "skyscrapers" and played a big part in Chicago's distinguished architectural history. Patrick earned his employers' approval when, through his uncle, he gained several architectural commissions for his firm.

Mike's best client was Chicago Joe Bohannon, who had questionable connections to the underworld. It was Joe who offered Patrick the chance to design a casino and resort hotel — an architect's dream project, which boosted his career into the big time. Still, his relationship with Joe had always been tenuous. Despite his desire to reform, Joe still couldn't shed his mob connections. Patrick was haunted by the thought that things could go wrong at any time.

Chet pondered all these factors, wondering if Patrick could balance this difficult challenge. Could he take on the restoration of this historic home, swing the finances, carry on his architectural business and solve another crime while all this was going on? He had his doubts. As Patrick's colleague, he depended upon their combined success. Chet had never put his finger on what drove him, what guided him and how he managed all his pressing obligations. Patrick acted, dreamed and took risks. It was Chet's job to worry, fix problems, and convince him to change direction if necessary.

Chapter Three

Only a half-hour had passed since Patrick's call. On this slow news day, the slaughter of a typical Chicago Saturday night hadn't yet begun. The police arrived promptly in full force: two uniforms, Detective Sergeant O'Malley and the coroner, also called the medical examiner. They should have brought a couple of construction laborers as well.

Patrick led the police to the basement and the grisly scene in the coal bin. O'Malley nodded to the patrolmen. As the lowest ranking members of the squad, they got the message, stripped off their tunics down to spotless white rayon shirts, cleared debris and took turns shoveling coal to expose the victim. After a time, while the two architects explained the furnace and the stoking conveyor called The Iron Fireman, the cops uncovered the body of a tall man in a charcoal suit, further encrusted with coal dust. His face smeared with dark blood caked on his forehead and nose, not even his mother would have recognized him. A shovel with dried blood on the blade lay beside the body. The two officers slipped the rotting corpse into a body bag.

"Make sure to check prints and DNA on all parts of the shovel," Patrick said, the metal and the wood."

"We'll handle the evidence," O'Malley objected. You probably tampered with it anyway."

"Put it in your notes and see if the blood matches the victim's DNA." Patrick persisted.

The medical examiner glared at him.

A policeman tagged the shovel and put it in a separate sack. The medical examiner snapped a few more photos of the victim and the scene, completed his notes and left. The detective instructed them to move their burden to a vehicle waiting outside.

Back in the entry hall, O'Malley grilled the members of the group. He already knew more about Patrick and Chet than he cared to remember. But he demanded to know what had brought them to this desolate, deserted place. When the realtor explained, he asked, "What else did you observe/" The detective knew Patrick too well to omit this question.

"You'll recall, Sergeant O'Malley, from our previous case together," Patrick said, "there were persons living at various times in that Victorian house in the next block used by the Detroit mob as a hideout."

"So, if you're so hot, what is your theory?" O'Malley asked.

"I'm not sure yet. Can't ruin some innocent guy's rep."

"You're so smart, what did he want? Nothing valuable here we can see."

"Who knows? Planting bugs, hiding loot — or something else.

"How come the vic was buried under all that coal?" O'Malley asked.

"Body's ripe — been there a while. Getting ready for winter. The previous owner told me they had ordered their winter supply. See that the window high in the wall of the basement? A dump truck backs into the driveway alongside the house. They stick a chute through the window, truck bed tips up, pours coal through an opening in the back panel, coal slides blindly into the bin. Covers the body."

"That figures," the detective said. "Know what killed him?"

"Can't be the coal — he would have had time to get out of the way." Patrick shrugged, spreading his palms. "Somebody breaks in, planning some kind of mischief. Owner or a squatter surprises him, grabs the shovel. Maybe he takes a swing at him in self-defense — forehead wound, bloody blade. Or maybe the perp attacks the owner."

"Yeah, yeah. But who was he?" O'Malley asked.

"Beats me."

"So much for your so-called sleuthing skills."

"Just what I need — a corpse. Probably put off the closing for months."

"Oh, Patrick, don't say that!" Kitty's eyes showed disappointment.

"It's alright, Kitty," Chet said. Although she knew Patrick well enough to win his heart, it might be years before she could penetrate the complex, mysterious workings of his mind. As much as he cared about architecture, his logic could stop him cold, and he would not rest until he solved the case.

O'Malley took down the realtor's contact information and closed his notebook. "That ought to do it. Watch out for this place, MacKenna."

"Was that fatherly advice or a threat?" The two of them had a history.

"You should forget about buying this dump, It may not be haunted, but it sure as hell is cursed — I smell more trouble."

"Maybe it's just as well," Chet said. "The delay will give you some time to investigate the property. Maybe you'll even cool off."

"You guys can go," the sergeant said, "We'll call you if we need anything else."

"We have to get this house!" Kitty said.

"I don't give up that easily," Patrick assured her. "But Chet's right. We have to look into these problems before we agree to the final contract. At the very least they're important negotiating points, which will affect the final price we pay."

"I just want to get started renovating our house," Kitty said.

"You hear that, Patrick?" Chet had no doubt what she wanted. "She said 'our house.'"

They headed toward Patrick's car, but the haunted look reappeared on his face. What was it Chet saw there? If he could understand it, his job would become easier.

He concluded it was not worry, but determination. Despite his young, hopeful eyes. chiseled features and a thick shock of dark brown hair over his sensitive face, Patrick had a knack for turning away all the demons that threatened him. He kept an eye on his vision.

Abigail locked the door and returned the key to the lockbox. She turned to face the street. The darkening sky released drops of fine rain, which turned into an impenetrable mist in the distance. She had again donned her immense coat against the chill and thrown the dark cowl over her head. Poised above the top step, her black clad silhouette, like a misplaced penguin, lurched toward her car and vanished into the fog-bound obscurity.

Chet watched the bleak caravan of realtor, ambulance and police van pull out of the street. He was concerned that Patrick, despite all these unresolved renovation issues. was still determined to buy this pack of trouble. First, they had to find out who was so interested in snooping around it. At the rate Patrick and Kitty were hurtling toward ownership of this ramshackle wreck, he figured they had better. And yet what about all that work waiting at the office on Monday morning?

Chet shrugged, as clueless as the police.

Chapter Four

When Patrick arrived at the new office the next morning, Chet was trying to help Yolanda manipulate an old switchboard.

"You found the new address this morning, Yolanda," Patrick said to the trim receptionist.

"Look at this old thing. What am I supposed to do with this?" She held up an ancient switchboard plug.

"I guess you'll learn how to play it," he said, "the way you play the rest of us."

"You'd better hope I do, or you'll start losing your so-called important business."

"Speaking of that," he continued. "Chet and I plan to drive out together to Joe Bohannon's meeting of their reorganized team at the Rockville site. You can hold our calls."

"I'll hold them, all right. What I can do with them is anybody's guess."

When it was time to leave for their meeting, Patrick sent Chet to the parking garage up the street to get the car, Briefcase in hand, as he passed Jason Holdroyd's door, his boss hailed him.

"Oh, there you are, Patrick. Come in here a minute."

Ooops, caught. A minute in Jason's reckoning could last an hour.

"Can't." He poked his head in the open doorway. "Just leaving to go to my construction meeting in Rockville."

"No matter, I just wanted to see how things are going with the new setup."

"Pretty well, I guess. We had to help Yolanda puzzle out old switchboard."

"You're pretty good at solving mysteries. Help is on the way on that score. The installers are due tomorrow to set up the new phone system."

He sat in the chair opposite Jason and set his case on the floor. This was going to take a while.

"Speaking of the casino resort, I hope you're focusing on the progress of the work out there — not finding any more bodies." His icy tone conveyed his usual disapproval of the client and his mob connections.

"Right. Combining the project visit with the Bohannon construction team meeting saves an extra trip." Patrick presented the facts as favorably as he could for Jason's benefit. "He's transferring project responsibility to his daughter Gloria and her husband Nick. Ultimately, they'll have full ownership, and he and his shady associates will have nothing to do with the project."

"Heading in the right direction, I suppose," Holdroyd said. "Will you send Chet in here please? I need to ask him how the staff are adjusting to the new space and equipment."

"Actually, he's waiting for me in front of the building. He went ahead to get out the car."

"He's going, too? How much money are we sending down this rat-hole?"

"I need to introduce him to the whole project team, and he's got a role in our presentation of the project's progress. Besides, they're paying us for every man-hour we spend." Patrick rose and headed for the door.

"Just let him know what I will expect. We have make our transition to the new space as smooth as possible and not let down any of our other paying clients."

At the curb at last, Patrick clambered into the passenger seat.

"Finally! That Irish cop said if I was still here when he came back, he'd run me in."

"Ah, wouldn't you know it?" Patrick declared in his broadest brogue. "He had to remind us of his singular importance in the traffic division of Chicago's finest."

"I ran out of excuses. I thought you'd never get down here."

"Sorry. Jason snagged me on the way out. He got in his usual dig on this project's drain on company resources. He expects us to help everyone adjust to the new space. At least the move seemed to cheer him up."

◊

At the jobsite Patrick and Chet climbed to the renovated second floor of the old farmhouse. Arriving at the meeting a few minutes early. they were greeted by Angela Atkins, a new employee for the casino resort, but an old friend of his.

"Hey Angela, getting used to the new routine?"

"For sure, Patrick, and I can't thank you enough."

"Don't mention it — after beating the odds downtown, you've earned a top job."

A late bloomer in her mid-thirties, to Patrick's critical eye, Angela still looked great. A few care lines marred her attractive face. A tailored grey business suit sheathed her handsome figure, but bright, quick eyes and alert demeanor were her most noticeable qualities. He was accustomed to greeting her with a pained look in his eyes, sympathetic to the simultaneous loss of her mother and a dear client and friend in the downtown murder case, but today he looked on with admiration. He had recommended her for this job, which enabled her to buy a car, get some new clothes and take better care of herself. She glanced back at Patrick and smiled from beneath trimmed bangs and bobbed brown hair.

When Gloria entered the room from her private office, Patrick felt his old longing return. His eyes locked on hers.. "How is young Michael doing?"

"You wouldn't believe it. He took his first steps, and he knows how to say, 'Mama.'"

"I wouldn't expect any less."

Chet pointed to the center seat he had saved, and Patrick took it.

Chicago Joe rapped on the conference table. "I'll now re-adjourn the meeting. Let's start."

Joe had a way with words. It wasn't Chet's way, nor that of anyone else he knew, but somehow this malaprop mobster managed to express himself.

"First, I'll remind you that in a couple of months I will be going away for a while, due to that deal I made with the feds. It's on that old sports betting rap and had nothing to do with my later activities. I'm counting on the rest of you to continue. The good news is that it speeds up my plan to turn the casino, hotel and music business over to my gorgeous and clever daughter Gloria, and her brainy husband Nick. The business will be totally free of the Outfit's confluence — strictly legit. It's my legal-see to her for putting up with me and the 'business' for her whole life so far.

"Gloria will take over the meeting. I've asked her to begin with a decryption of how she up-to-dated this farmhouse to its good old-fashioned look. Then Nick will fill us in on finishing off the hotel and casino apportionances and all their prerequisite electrical connections, not forgetting of course future plans to expend the project. "It's all yours, Gloria."

"Thanks, Pop. You all know our office manager Angela Atkins, my right hand, whom we met during our architect Patrick's previous murder case. I'm happy to announce that we have named Angela Secretary of the new hotel casino corporation. She will be taking notes of this meeting." Angela raised her pen and smiled toward the group.

"This house project required some changes in building layout," Gloria continued, waving an arm in a circle to include their present meeting space. "Upstairs we created this modern, air-conditioned conference room and offices. On the exterior we matched historical materials for a new roof, new siding with the weathered wood look and repairs to the original porches and windows. We restored the parlor until it recaptured its 1890s charm, refurbishing the original Victorian wing chairs, sofas, piecrust tables and Tiffany lamps." Borrowing Jackie Kennedy's phrase she added, "We decided to leave the main floor it exactly like it was."

When it was Nick McGurk's turn to talk, he summarized his work from its very early stages a year earlier. This included helping engineersspecify gambling equipment, install electrical connections in an unobtrusive way, and design lighting, video, communications, alarm systems for the offices and a remote casino control room. Nick has overseen planning for the marina and dockside theme restaurant, and an island teahouse, which would also serve as a stage for musical events. Patrick, please fill us in on your progress with plans for these projects."

"To back up a bit," Patrick began, "we took our cue from Joe's love of music and all his many contacts in the industry. I suggested we open up the resort to visitors from the river, work a marina into the design, and place the concert venue along that creek. On an island in this enlarged inlet, it will serve daily as a teahouse, which can be used for special events, weddings and conferences, and easily converted into a stage for rock concerts.

"This project is being directed by me and my capable business partner, Chet Nuezing, whom most of you have met."

Chet set up the presentation boards on two easels and changed them as Patrick spoke.

"Here's the site plan for the improvements and an aerial perspective rendering of the completed marina-resort complex.

"Along the riverfront and in the widened inlet." Patrick said, "we'll have slips for the temporary and permanent mooring of pleasure craft, to attract visitors from up and down the river to the casino and special concerts. The teahouse will have glass walls, which will slide out of the way to convert into a stage and yet can be closed up for year-round events and restaurant service."

"How are you progressing on the bidding?" Nick asked.

"Construction documents for the civil engineering and bidding are complete for the work to create the widened inlet and island. We're asking for bids and have set a deadline of next Friday."When will it be theasible to schedule the grand opening concert?" Chicago Joe asked.

"Construction is nearly complete for the hotel, casino, and restaurants. Then over the winter we'll complete working drawings and specifications for the stage, teahouse, and marina structures. In spring we'll build them. We should be, in a position to have a grand opening concert by summer."

"Got all that, Angela?" Nick asked. She nodded.

"Patrick, are you going to leave us some photos of those fancy renditionings? Joe asked.

"Here are copies of all the renderings we've shown today with our description of the project." Chet handed out booklets of what he had just presented.

"Fantastic!" Joe said, "

"All it will take, Joe," Nick continued, "is for you to okay all this and get the money flowing — for Patrick's team and the civil contractor. "

"The check's in the mail, as they say." He chuckled and smiled at Patrick. "You lead the way, and we'll precede."

◊

Nick continued his long narrative on the project's history. Her father's mention of a check reminded Gloria of the first steps they took a year earlier. Joe was a firm believer in his cash system, which employed various methods of collection, some firmer than others. Cash was harder to trace, and it was the mainstay of mob survival.

Even though checks were commonly used in business, Joe still found his cash system very useful and never completely abandoned it. His cash could bring good luck, like the time when Joe and Gloria appeared in mid-morning at the county courthouse to make the zoning application. They were told to see Tubman Balquier, County Clerk, whom Gloria anticipated to be a bumpkin, attired in an apron and green visor, like the counterman at the local feed store. When they entered his domain of wood paneling, however, they found a crackling fireplace and an American flag. Seated behind an oversized desk, was a country gentleman. He hoisted his substantial bulk and offered a glad hand.

"Howdy, I'm Tubby Balquier." He pronounced it balky-er. Joe took his hand readily and introduced himself and Gloria as proprietors of the old farm estate.

Joe recognized the surname — of one of the founding families in these parts. He wore a black suit and a gray sateen vest covering a substantial paunch,

"I see in the paper you've got big plans for the old farm estate," the County Clerk said.

"Yep," Joe replied, "that's what brings us here today."

"You've come to the right place. While our Plan Commission and Council approve such things, this office is where you start and finish most permits.

Peering at Joe through his octagonal rimless spectacles, he handed Joe several forms, which he passed to his daughter. Gloria began them filling out, while this official asked Joe questions about such details of the property as: water source, well water testing, soil type and, oddly, "How many draft animals on the property?"

"I thought they got rid of the draft in 1973," Gloria said.

"Not that kind of a draft, sweetheart," he explained. "He means pulling plows and such." He and Tubby had a good laugh over that one.

"When was this ordinance written, anyway?" Gloria asked.

The bespectacled clerk checked the title page of his ordinances book. "In 1923. We had one of the first zoning ordinances in the country!"

"In fact we do have some animals," Joe said, "a pair of donkeys, Stubby and Ornery, and Billy, our goat—for herbiage control, you know?"

"Naturally," said the County Clerk. "Now, with your filing fee of a thousand dollars — that's twenty dollars an acre for the fifty acres involved — I will file this, and we can set a hearing date."

"Of course." Joe pulled out a roll of bills and peeled off ten Hamiltons,

"Oh, you don't actually pay for it until your hearing date is set. It wouldn't be fair to tie up your cash. Until then you only need to provide a check to be filed with your application."

"Um, didn't bring any checks. I'll have to get back to you on that."

"Just send us the check whenever you have it, and we'll consider your filing complete," Joe reached for his pocket to put the money away. The County Clerk placed a restraining hand on Joe's arm, adding. "Although, if you'd like to cut down the delay — I can offer you our expedited option; a thousand additional cash. I'm up for reelection next year, you know."

"Of course," He handed the bills over to the County Clerk. Gloria suppressed a sly grin.

The County Clerk grunted with satisfaction and consulted his Rolex "About time for my dinner." He smiled. "That should wrap it up."

On their way out of the County office Joe remarked to Gloria, "I know this rigmarole is tedious, but it's all part of setting up a legitimate business."

Gloria shrugged and smiled to herself. "Whatever, Pop. Still learning."

What really had happened to get the cash flowing was for Nick to deposit half of his working capital to open a new checking account. This step was initiated at the urging of Patrick, Angela and Nick, to comply with the federal law regulating large cash deposits, which triggered federal reporting requirements. Although Nick had opened it with cash purloined during his clandestine departure from the Detroit mob, these capital infusions were due to his genius for turning a profit. In this case he pooled some of the original money he had skimmed from Detroit in his frustration over the absence of a promotion. He later added proceeds of his thriving chain of laundromats, Mommy Laundry. Now Angela could write checks and Gloria or Nick could sign them, like any normal business. This was only Step One in Gloria's and Nick's plan to make this operation legitimate.

The matter of opening a checking account had been bandied back and forth between Joe and the office of his downtown attorneys, Franklin and Sligh. For years his longtime ally, counsel and friend in a pinch. Jonathan Sligh had been urging him to set up banking capabilities.

◊

As these recollections faded from her mind, the voice of their secretary caught her attention, and she refocused on the progress of their project reorganization meeting. Angela mentioned a few future agenda items and set the date of the next meeting. Joe declared their business complete and "re-adjourned" the meeting.

As everyone filed out, Nick pulled Patrick aside.

"Hey, I'm still not out from under the Detroit mob. Jimmy Romo wants Marco Candicci on our project management team."

"That's why Joe Bohannon is taking his time to let go. He's not scheduled to report to the Arizona farm for another two months. He wants to use the time to make sure you and Gloria are fully in charge before he releases control."

"I don't trust Marco Candicci — he already seems to know too much about what we've decided, and I don't know where he's getting his information."

"Hmm, I wonder if he's planted bugs in that house we're trying to buy. There are so many strange noises. It's as if when we work there, we're not really alone."

"How could you find out?"

"I'll make a thorough inspection over the weekend. You available, Chet?"

Chet was looking forward to the simple pleasures of a weekend with his family. The kind with no immediate worries except getting the kids to their various sporting events and rounding everyone up at mealtimes. Concerned for his mentor and friend, however, he agreed to join Patrick on Saturday for a thorough inspection of the Victorian horror. His only remaining hope was that they could finish what they had to do on Saturday, so he could salvage enough time to enjoy Sunday dinner and the comforts of home.

"Saturday morning anyway." Chet didn't very often get roped into obligations in front of clients, so he forgave Patrick for his blackmail — this one time anyway. "Not a problem."

◊

When Patrick and Chet arrived back at the new office that afternoon, Yolanda was struggling with a new "communications console." She sat at the helm, an impressive U-shaped affair with an array of buttons for telephone and intercom control.

"We're back. Good afternoon!'

"What's good about it?" she said. "Look at this monstrosity! Some clown just rolled it in here on a dolly. He supposedly hooked it up, but I can't even answer the phone."

"Well, if your knowledge is half as good as your superior attitude, I'm sure you'll have it working in no time."

"You'd better hope I do, or you'll start losing business."

This was one of many challenges in the firm's new space in a downtown office building closer to the heart of the loop. Last Friday, the century old firm of Holdroyd & Robb had required the staff to pack their tools, memorabilia and key project data in file boxes, put them on top of their desks to be unpacked in their new downtown location Monday morning. On each new desk sat a chunky monitor, which faced a more traditional drafting board, just in case, with a traditional T-square or parallel bar, drafting triangles and the other paraphernalia used for laying out plans and creating new ones.

At the old place draftsmen, some with green eyeshades and aprons, had used these implements to create their drawings in ink or pencil, first on starched linen, and in later years on mylar. On bath towel-sized sheets they had delineated many of the great skyscrapers, now considered mid-rise buildings of twenty stories or more; Their walls of masonry and glass were hung on iron and steel frames rather than supporting the entire structure, aptly described as "curtain walls." Now younger draftsman would create portions of each large image of such drawings on computer screens, under the watchful eyes of the old timers, who knew how the building parts should be put together.

In these times of lightning speed technological change, where hundred-year-old traditions vanish overnight, Patrick was counting on the persistence of people. In the reception area of this new office the chairs were more, comfortable, and new framed photos of larger, more recent buildings graced the walls. Yet all comers were still hosted by the quick-witted and attractive Yolanda, her clear blue eyes and clipped speech revealing her central European lineage. Her manner was strictly American, though, brusque and witty, with courtesy for clients and crankiness or sarcasm for others, as she saw fit.

Jason Holdroyd's loyal secretary still occupied a desk outside his office, ever hopeful of receiving tidbits of praise or good cheer from the boss she had not-so-secretly loved for years. Roger Baird, the firm's chief specification writer, displayed a framed degree from Yale on his wall. He still cut and pasted the correct language to describe each material to be used on a project — its quality, composition and established standards it must meet. A young scribe would take over, find the exact words and paragraphs in the electronic archives and magically transport them into a screen image of the pages in the final printed book.

Chet 's office next to his had one window looking outdoors at the scene and, on its other side, a glass partition overlooking a sea of workstations with adjacent drafting desks, where project architects and engineers and their assistants designed and described the appearance, function and assembly of all the building components.

These drawings included floor plans, elevations — front views of exterior and interior walls — and cross-sectional views of all major intersections of walls, floors and interior partitions within the structures.

Patrick MacKenna had scored a corner office. Outside of his window this time, instead of screeching, right-angle turns of the elevated trains, he could look down at a busy intersection or up a few stories in the canyon of office windows to open sky.

While conditions, budgets, and society changed radically, the people persisted. Their personalities, daily lives, and adventures continued as an unending source of casual conversation,

And so, the people at the historic firm looked forward haltingly, bravely feeling their into the future.

Chapter Five

The two architects met at the house property on Saturday morning. As Patrick inspected a pipe that disappeared into a hollow plumbing chase wall, he heard thumping and footsteps coming from elsewhere in the house.

"I wish we had been able to turn up a set of house plans," Patrick said.

"I searched City Hall records and found nothing," Chet said. "I checked with the architectural firm that originally designed several houses on this block, but they don't have this one."

First however, they split up and searched for listening devices in the most obvious places. When they found none, they met back in the bedroom.

"Hey, what's that sound?" Chet heard thumping and footsteps.

Patrick dropped his pencil and listened. "Let's investigate. Meanwhile, let's also keep checking for hidden bugs." He ran upstairs and down, looking for source, while Chet carefully inspected the bedroom floor, surfaces, niches, lamps and other unobtrusive objects in hopes of finding a listening device. After a half-hour they gave up the unproductive search.

"When you think about it, it seems our problem is more direct than that," Patrick said. "Who needs a bug when he can listen from a hidden passage behind a wall?"

"The best way to find any hidden rooms or passages in the house," Chet suggested, is to create an interior floor plan from scratch. Then we can compare it with the measured exterior dimensions of the house."

"It makes today's project all the more urgent."

Chet. took out his twenty-foot tape and began sketching wall locations and dimensions between them on his clipboard.

They cleared and dusted a Victorian writing table in the bedroom window alcove to use as a drafting board. Patrick plopped down his oversized quadrille drawing pad, and Patrick laid out a freehand floor plan from the sheets of notes Chet provided. Occasionally he would doodle in the margins of the drawing, an idea for how an interior room should look, a list of cabinetry and equipment to be placed in the space, or a plan view of each window, door or wall.

Watching Patrick sketch had always fascinated him. Sitting down, he would stretch out his arms to shoot back his sleeves, stretch his shoulders, and smooth the yellow buff tracing paper from a roll held in his left hand over an image. Then he would draw the revised layout on the overlay and slide it beneath its new location, and inscribe the revised arrangement in place of the old one.

If it were a conceptual drawing, often he would start with geometric shapes in three dimensions. For an aerial view of an entire project, he would set out the site boundaries with roads, creeks, wooded areas and blocks representing building groups, sometimes adding another layer of tracing paper so he could move the building group around on the site. Then he would make a final sketch that included plazas, walks, trails roads and the final building arrangement and begin filling in selected details in the foreground, such as windows, roofs, building entryways and the larger landscape elements — tree groups, shrubbery and water features.

For an eye level view, his perspective would be lower and would include foreground objects, such as a tree branch, a building edge or a person walking toward the place, and a converging view of the street, corridor or room being depicted. His many years of drawing and painting had taught him how to convert the three-dimensional vision he saw in his mind to a flat drawing on paper, and sometimes add color to increase realistic effect. His visualization skills had distinguished him in the office and established his talent for involving other people — colleagues, clients and contractors — to see how their final projects would look.

But today Patrick sketched from each page of notes Chet handed him and noted dimensions and walls as his master floor plan drawing of the bedroom level took shape..

As they worked, Chet asked him about the case.

"Patrick, who do you suspect as the murder victim? If you tell me what you wouldn't tell Detective O'Malley, maybe it will give us an idea."

"Possible suspects, First, there was Bulldog Dugan. Heavyset and muscular, he seldom wore anything better than jeans and a Detroit Pistons T-shirt. He had an elaborate tattoo spelling MOTHER on his right arm. He was a spy from the Detroit outfit, sent here to infiltrate Joe Bohannon's North Side mob. But we convicted him as an accessory to murder of the downtown attorney and put him in the pen. The actual perp got away and is still at large."

"There was that disgruntled employee Tom from our architectural office." Chet added, "who quit and started working for Bulldog. He got off with time served and probation under our firm's supervision. But he hasn't been showing up at work lately. He has never worn anything better than wash pants and a hoodie in his life. Besides, this victim is much taller than Tom, and, despite the grime on his face, I could see his features are different."

"The only other one living in the next block was Marco Candicci, an enforcer for Jimmy Romo, the mob boss in Detroit. They have never been able to nail him for the hit job on that downtown lawyer. When the results come back they compare the DNA in his bedroom in the other house with that of this body. He's in town to pester Nick, but what would he be doing over here?"

"What if the owner appeared suddenly," Chet asked, "then surprised him in the coal bin and attacked him with the shovel? Wouldn't Candicci put up a fight and win? What if it was the former owner lying there, and Candicci caused his death?

"Charles Simmons was tall enough, and he could have come directly from work, explaining the suit, But you're right about the DNA, Once the lab results come back, O'Malley will let us know whose prints are is on the shovel handle and whose blood is on the blade."

As Chet waited for Patrick to catch up on drawing his measurements, he inspected and cleaned out a clogged lavatory drain that disappeared into a hollow plumbing chase wall.

They finished up a floor plan of the bedroom level, a pretty good morning's work. But for this laborious process, Patrick said he would need more help. This time Chet didn't speak.

Chapter Six

Three days later, Patrick needed to visit the job site to coordinate work with the grading contractor, When Gloria learned he was coming out to the project office that afternoon, she abandoned the budget she was studying at her desk, sighed and slumped in her executive chair.

The prospect of seeing him awakened old feelings. Her mind drifted back to their separation for her European tour.

While Joe had stayed home to deal with the complex problems of launching the casino and hotel, working with the bankers, architects, engineers, lawyers and contractors involved, he had sent Gloria and her mother on a grand tour of Europe. The trip was the long-postponed "vacation," he had promised his wife Candy for many years — he had never been able to break free from the stressful, guarded stance he had to take to maintain his position. Candy appreciated the change of scene after enduring his violent years running organized crime. When Patrick became engaged to Kitty, Gloria hoped the trip would help deal with the problems she faced and fill a big hole in her life.

She'd explained to her friends that the distance and distraction would help prepare her to make a fresh start and get a second chance at romance. Privately, she felt it would shield her from other concerns arising from their breakup. She needed time to think.

She had met Nick McGurk a considerable time before her voyage. When a thunderstorm disrupted the grand groundbreaking ceremony for the project, the criminal element had taken advantage of the confusion and kidnapped her. Nick had protected her and finally freed her from the grip of criminals, ironically, with Patrick's help. She found it hard to hate any of the flawed men in her life.

Nick McGurk had come along at a good time. A fugitive from organized crime himself, he had escaped from the mob through a clever plot, while he got satisfying revenge against Jimmy Romo for his failure to reward his valuable assistance. According to his own account, the Detroit mob boss had taken his dedicated service for granted, murdered his brother, and refused to help his hard-working, grieving, and ailing mother.

Rising from cruel, even desperate circumstances, Nick looked up to Gloria's refinement, her prosperous family's elegant lifestyle. and her unmatched beauty. Unlike any man she had ever met other than her father, he gave her his worshipful respect, love, and devotion. She and Nick shared the goal of escaping the dictates of mob bosses and earning their way on their own merits.

Upon her return, she was thrilled when Nick proposed to her. He was devoted to her beyond all reason. After her miraculous rescue, she trusted him to look out for her at all costs. At the same altar where she would promise to love, honor, and respect him she pledged to the Virgin Mary never to let Patrick into her personal life again. And she was a woman of her word.

But as the inheritor of Joe's project, she was now required to work with Patrick on a regular basis. Together they must finish creating the project to house their new business enterprise. Her pain in enduring this frequent close contact was hard to conceal, yet it was evident in her unsmiling face. Her downcast eyes were unable to engage with his own, which she had once adored. There were other bonds, too painful to face, which made her anguish almost unbearable.

When Patrick arrived, he headed straight for Gloria's office. She steeled herself and greeted him. "Yes, Patrick. What is it?"

"Just wanted to check in and let you know I'm here to coordinate some technical matters with Nick."

"Okay, thank you."

"And I just wanted to apologize for last week."

"Apologize?"

"Well, I gushed about little Mike. I guess such things don't belong in a business meeting."

"It wasn't that noticeable. I'll have to admit, I admire him. He's a tough little tyke." She looked away.

"Right. Anyway, Nick and I have to talk about grading and a few business details."

"You'll find him in the construction trailer."

And so it went. Gloria sighed and returned to studying her budget report.

◊

Patrick sat in Nick's trailer and reported what he and Kitty had discovered at the Victorian house over the weekend.

"So, you don't think the victim was Marco Candicci?"

"Not unless you believe in ghosts," Patrick added. "Marco is still with us, stonewalling. It's no surprise he wasn't forthcoming about the identity of the body."

"I guess I wouldn't be, either, if I had knocked him off."

"He must be the one haunting us, not concerned about being discovered in the house. He would have a lot of spying opportunities he with all those hidden passages."

"At least that would explain how he knows so much about your doings."

"Oh, by the way, I forgot to mention, I discovered a rear door on the side of the tower, covered in brick and matching the adjacent foundation. I thought it was merely a blocked-up window opening, but it's a secret entrance to the tower stairs."

"So, he can sneak in and out without detection," Nick said, "even while the house is occupied."

"It's a good thing I got in and discovered that."

"What's in that house, anyway?"

"I haven't stopped looking. I'd sure like to get the goods on them."

"You might find out what plans the Detroit operation has for us."

"For sure, I'll keep looking into that. Anything turns up, I'll let you know."

Chapter Seven

Kitty set out on a bright Wednesday morning and drove the now familiar route to the Victorian house. Because of the murder, Patrick warned her never to enter the house alone. But she was burning with ideas for renovation and eager to check conditions on site. She wanted to evaluate the house in daylight to begin planning the reuse program for their new home. Growing up in Ireland, she wasn't afraid to confront spirits. Maybe she could make this ghost back off and leave them alone.

She left the interstate, crossed the river and headed northwest on the diagonal artery, Milwaukee Avenue. She wound her way through the neighborhood to the old estates on Bond Street. In the early chill of fall street trees were turning yellow, brilliant orange and brown, adding seasonal charm to the once distinguished setting. With the key from the lockbox she entered.

Morning sun penetrated the large, dusty windowpanes, found color in the layers of grime on oriental rugs, and set natural wood tones aglow. She imagined people living in the unaltered and long unused parlor and dining room in earlier times. A couple of small rooms renovated by previous owners were stripped of their molding, ornament and fine wood paneling, in a clumsy attempt to make them look modern. The kitchen and breakfast areas were straight out of the 1950s, fitted out with all the latest features and labor-saving devices of the postwar era — a breakfast bar with one rounded end, the other end connecting to a wall counter. A double bowl ceramic sink with a garbage disposal set in one of the drains. A white porcelain Magic Chef gas range with streamlined chrome handles, and a vintage model electric dishwasher. Enameled metal cabinets with rounded door edges and streamlined door and drawer pulls dated from the last modernization. State-of-the-art in 1950, it still served the current owners up to the present day. The style was historical in its own way. Economics dictated it would have to do for another couple of years.

Most rooms had removable wood storm windows, with screen panels stored in the basement, which had to be exchanged twice a year with the seasons. The third floor and stair tower seemed like a fairy castle for an imprisoned princess. In fact, as Kitty entered each room, vibrations from the past took her to a different era.

She spent over an hour touring and evaluating the rooms on the main and second floors, taking pictures with her small digital camera. She dusted a chair and sat down at the kitchen table to write her conclusions. For each room she listed conditions in three categories: acceptable, top renovation priority, and long-term restoration potential.

She heard bumping and rattling noises with no visible source in the room. At first she attributed them to trucks rumbling up and down the street outside. Then they seemed closer, from above. She climbed the main stairway to the third floor, where it was very dark. The apartment's rooms had small dormer windows, made even darker by thick velvet curtains. She noticed the closet door open and walked over to close it. But she found it led into a small hallway. On the right was the doorway to the stair tower, which they had climbed on their first tour. Through the back of the closet, beyond a false sliding back panel, was a second bedroom. It was dark but she entered anyway.

The odor of stale cigarette smoke lingered in the stuffy attic room. A few rays of daylight struggled dimly through a narrow crack between closed velvet curtains. As her eyes adjusted, there loomed the vague outline of a large male form. He aimed a flashlight at the contents of drawers, under the bed and within the closet. She stumbled on a box and made a noise. Silently cursing her clumsiness, she froze.

The figure turned and faced in her direction. She made out the shadowy shape of a tall, stocky man. Her heart pounding, she spoke to the specter. "Oh spirit, how have we offended thee?"

"What the f — !" The beast bellowed. With a sardonic laugh, it replied in kind, "Oh intruder, you have indeed insulted us. We are guardians of the history and protectors of our Master's rightful property."

Her bravado evaporated along with the spirit. Kitty screamed and retreated a few steps toward the closet where she had entered. "Wha-what do you wish us to do to r -r-remove the spell you have cast on this place?" She spoke with what breath she had left.

"Abandon this house forever!" The looming figure spread his arms for emphasis.

Terrified, she retraced her path through the attic to the main stairway. She'd seen quite enough of the spirits of the place for one day. Gathering up her notes, she secured the house and drove back home to Lake Shore Drive.

That evening she told Patrick she had ignored his warning in order to tackle the work of renovation. She said merely that she had given a lot of thought to the renovations and showed him her priority list.

"It would be expensive to change over all these decors to a common theme." he said.

"We can live with it as is for a while. I'm not worried about the 1950s kitchen. But . . ." She let the thought trail off and let him ramble on. How could she tell him what she had seen?

"What should we do with such a mélange of periods and styles?" Patrick persisted. "What if we keep the period style of each and enhance it, and keep alive the home's mystery?"

"Oh, there's plenty of mystery in that house," she said. "I met up with some kind of phantom in the house today," she blurted. "I told that spirit we wanted to rid ourselves of his spell on the house. He told me the only way would be to abandon it!"

"Oh crap," Patrick said. "That was no spirit. It was someone trying to scare you off. He may be a violent criminal."

"He succeeded. I ran out immediately and came home. He didn't seem human. This monster even spoke to me like a spirit."

"Did he now?" Patrick said, mimicking the high-pitched ironic brogue of his father Seamus. "We'll have to organize a little visit and stay there until we can smoke him out."

Chapter Eight

The tall man paced the secret attic room like a caged animal. He punched a number on his cell phone and kept it on speaker. While it rang he looked around the quiet office he had set up for himself in the secret room. It had all the ornate decor of the past and a few relics of the elaborate furnishings that had been stored up there. He parted the curtains, but the smoke curling around his head temporarily obscured his view of the distant scene

He was always nervous when he called Jimmy, kingpin of the Detroit operations. The connection was always tenuous, readily cut off when his boss became impatient. It would also be hard to hear, because of the voice processor and white noise interference he used to obscure the conversation from any unwanted listener. He punched in the number. While he waited, he inhaled his filter-tip Winston and let it out slowly. "Cancer — ha!" he muttered, Dying of cancer was as laughable as it was unlikely for someone in his business—

A burst of static came over the line and and then a gruff voice, "Yeah?"

"Jimmy?"

"Marco… crackle, ROAR…What?"

"Little issue with our plan for Joe's operations. that's all."

"Better speed it up. Pretty soon Joe has to start his extended vacation You and his daughter Gloria are taking over."

"He's sure taking his time about it. The thing is, I'm having trouble getting back inside. They keep having these meetings to organize the casino and hotel management and pass it on to Gloria. I'm still waiting for my invitation."

"It's a problem, but Joe and I go way back. He just wants to be sure of you. Have you done what— Another CRASH and CRACKLE muddled the audio. "…cleaned out the safe yet?"

"Still working on it. Every time I try to get in there, these buyers are sending someone to inspect or exploring it themselves."

"Now you listen to this: You get the contents of that safe, NOW, and you know why. No more crap, or you're fin…CRASH, ROAR, MORE STATIC…and dead meat."

"I hear you loud and clear."

Another roar and more static obscured his final words. The final crash, though, was the sound of Jimmy Romo hanging up the phone.

Cool Marco was sweating. He loosened his tie and tapped another cigarette out of the pack, ignited it with his pocket lighter and took a couple of nervous puffs. Then he snubbed it out and stood up.

He looked out the window to the street. Damn, there was the Honda again, pulling onto the driveway. Presently, he heard noises in the bedroom below. He decided things were getting too hot to handle in his private sanctum. He'd better retreat for his own safety and return another day.

◊

When Patrick returned home for the weekend, Kitty suggested they visit the house on Sunday to explore and visualize how they would occupy its many rooms. Patrick welcomed the chance to spot check his new floor plans and to find and confront the so-called spirit Kitty had faced. They arrived at about ten in the morning and climbed to the bedroom.

Patrick roamed the house to verify dimensions on the floor plans and make a quick check of the rooms to see if they were alone in the house. Kitty entered the hidden system from the closet door they had found in the bedroom. Despite Patrick's warnings, she was determined to spy on the mysterious stranger in the attic and thought she could do so without detection. When she reached the servants' attic on the third floor, she found that the route to the rooms ended in a small closet. Through a crack in the door she could hear the squeak of floorboards, thumping sounds and the footsteps. Peering through the crack she looked for the source of these noises.

The room with the spirit, however, was silent. The chair was empty, the smoke dissipated, and only the smell of stale cigarette smoke and old wood lingered in the room. The ashtray beside the chair, previously full of cigarette butts, was empty — and wiped clean. She wondered whether the man she had seen here before was real or a figment of her imagination.

She tried not to move, afraid to miss something if she broke the silence. A rush of air and whooshing sound disturbed the peace. "Oooh Cedric, is the coost clear-r-r?" A woman's voice with a strong brogue pierced the silence. In the heavily curtained attic, the only light was a dim glow supplied by two tapered candles, no doubt carelessly left burning in its missing occupant's hasty departure. The old-fashioned tapers emitted feeble rays and smoke, which materialized into to the wispy figure of a tall, slender man before her eyes.

"Ay, the intruder has abandoned our trysting place — it is safe." The phantom said.

Smoke from of the second candle transformed to a head capped with a white maid's bonnet, followed by the lower body, wearing a white apron over a black dress. She appeared young, with sparkling dark eyes and a radiant smile. The man, in a butler's white shirt, sleeves rolled up, and dark trousers with a satin stripe up the side, appeared dashing and handsome. The couple embraced.

Kitty peered from her closet vantage in open-mouthed amazement at the unfolding scene. She strained to hear their whispered speech.

"Will Claudia miss you?" the woman whispered.

"Nay, she sleeps in her prison graveyard as we speak. She'll not bother us again."

"Together at last!"

"Ay, but we now have the living to contend with," the suitor declared. "First the criminal, and now some deluded Irish folk who wish to settle here."

"Will we ever have peace?" the female phantom asked.

"Not until we are freed from this scene, by destruction of this cursed place,"

"'Twill be sad," she said, "But for this house, we might never have met."

"And yet 'tis the scene of our undoing."

Kitty could restrain herself no longer. She stepped forth. "Beloved and loving spirits, 'tis I, Kitty O'Connor MacKenna, of County Cork born, here to witness and bless your union."

The woman spoke. "Kitty, our dear sister, we would love and honor ye as well, and yet we both must heed the wise counsel of my lover Cedric. What say ye, me darlin'?"

"Tell me of this place." Kitty said. "May we live here with our family? You would of course be welcome."

"I echo the kind greetings of me beloved Aurora" Cedric responded, "but it is not for us to say. You have heard my fears. If we were freed, disaster would befall its inhabitants. Beware... beware..."

The voice trailed off and the specters dissolved into the musty darkness.

Carefully she extinguished the tapers. She returned to the bedroom wondering what to tell Patrick of her strange encounter.

◊

After Kitty left to check the rooms, Patrick returned to the bedroom chamber and studied the wall behind the four-poster bed, on either side of which hung elaborately framed oil paintings of an owner's ancestor and his wife. When he stared at the man's image, its eyes stared back at him. He'd had this experience before and found that a skillful painter can place the eyes of his subject such that, no matter where the viewer is in the room, he can't escape the subject's gaze. As he walked about to test this theory, the painting slipped on its hanger wire and tilted. That was harder to explain than the eyes. Was the subject of the portrait trying to tell him something?

He reached for the frame and explored with his hand behind it for the hooks that engaged the hanger wire. The wall was not flat. It felt cold, like steel. He carefully lifted off the man's picture, where he discovered a safe embedded in the wall. It had a simple round dial with a pointer to single digits from 1 to 10 embossed on the steel surface. Patrick tried entering month-and-year combinations, the street number of the house, all zeros, and other easily guessed combinations, without success. Wondering if this might explain Candicci's obsession with the house, he paused to think. He reflected on Chicago's gangster history and recalled Al Capone's final days of freedom. On a hunch he entered the year he had been sent to prison, 1-9-3-0, reversing direction of the dial after each digit. A loud click signaled the release of internal bolts. Patrick pushed the handle downward and swung open a thick steel door.

The interior enclosure was about two feet across, three feet high and two feet deep. He was surprised that, despite some dirt, the metal parts of the ancient safe still worked so smoothly. Indeed, on the top shelf he found a familiar blue and yellow can of WD-40 and caught a hint of the sicky-sweet smell of the spray, commonly used to free up rusted metal parts. On a middle shelf sat several stacks of hundred-dollar bills bound with paper collars in stacks of fifty bills. He chose not to upset the spirits of the house and left those in place. At the bottom of the safe, amid accumulated dust, crumbs of plaster and soot rested two old-fashioned ledger books, covered in faded blue canvas, with burgundy leather spines and front corners. Next to them was a more recent bound journal, a school notebook with a black-and-white spattered cover design, containing To Do lists from recent years up to the present. Patrick removed the ledgers and the notebook, put them in his canvas backpack and locked the safe. He wiped the face of the door and the dial with his handkerchief to clean off his prints.

When Kitty rejoined him, she was bursting with news but considered the most credible way to present her discovery to Patrick.

"What did you find up there?" he asked.

"No sign of that smoking fiend. I'm beginning to wonder if he were ever there."

"Maybe not. Find any ghosts?"

"Just the usual suspects — spirits of the dead lovers, and so on." Her mother always insisted she tell the truth.

"Thank goodness," he said, not giving it another thought. "We've got enough problems already."

They had each collected plenty of information and decided to call it a day, They planned and come back with reinforcements, namely Chet, next week.

Before leaving, the two of them made a final check of the basement. Patrick had left open the window to the coal bin, and the stink of death was mostly abated by the crisp fall air. At the other end of the basement, they inspected storage rooms with masonry walls and solid doors. In one, some empty Mason jars remained from storage of canned fruit, but the shelves held nothing else.

The second room was the wine cellar, its floor strewn with fragments of broken glass and cubbyholes with dozens of bottles still aging on their racks. While many of the labels had deteriorated with time and were unreadable, Patrick found a dozen more dark green bottles with their trademark brand name embossed in the glass. He recalled Simmons's promise of this tempting perk of ownership as a further incentive, although for the couple certainly not a deciding one. He surveyed the room again and noticed for the first time that a small table with an inlaid ivory and ebony chessboard sat toward the back of the space. two chairs occupied opposite sides of the tabletop, supported by elaborate Ionic scrollwork legs, Matching ivory and ebony chess men were set up for a game. Curiously, unlike every other object in the room, there was no film of dust on the playing surface. He thought it odd that he had not noticed this unique feature on his first visit. But he attributed this to his greater interest in this motivated seller and their discussion of fine wine.

Patrick poked wood supports, floor joists and masonry walls, a prelude to more thorough interior testing of walls, ceilings and basement features they would have to do in the final inspection This would be necessary before they estimated renovation cost just to make the building habitable, restore basic building systems to operable condition, and begin to figure out the cost of building restoration. He sighed heavily, glad that they must postpone this work to another day.

Chapter Nine

Back home, Kitty put her meat pie casserole in the oven, poured a beer for each of them and sat down opposite Patrick in their living area. The twilight faded and the few craft visible on the blackening lake twinkled in the distance.

"That was a good day's work," Patrick said. "We've got a pretty good idea of what it will take to occupy that house."

"I guess so," Kitty said.

"You guess? What's the problem?"

"Oh, nothing you would understand."

"What's that supposed to mean?"

"Well, you'll think I'm crazy if I tell you this."

"Believe me, I always try my best to understand you."

"Well," Kitty said, "there is more going on in that attic than that phony spirit, the gangster. There are some real spirits up there. I saw them materialize. Many years ago they used that attic bedroom for their secret love affair."

"How did you know they were really spirits?"

"Oh, I have seen such phantoms before, in the old country."

"How did they appear?" Patrick was careful to respect what Kitty said she observed.

"Their forms took shape in puffs of smoke in the darkened attic They were quaint in their dress and speech, from early in the previous century. She wore the costume of a house servant, he the more formal attire of a butler and valet. As they talked to each other, they resented the presence of that criminal and said we also were disturbing their peace. I then stepped forward from my hiding place and spoke to them. They were most cordial. She looked up. "Are you still with me?"

"Yes — I'm beginning to think anything is possible in that place."

"They welcomed us and said they would respect and love us as their countrymen, except that—"

"Except what?"

"… that we are deluded to think the house is suitable to live in."

Patrick was silent for a moment. Her story had such realistic, plausible details that it must be true. He was fascinated to learn what these beings from another time looked like, said, and did.

"My god! I have a bit of a confession to make to you as well. The eyes of the man's portrait were following me. Then the picture shifted on the wall. I removed it and found a wall safe behind it, full of cash and ledgers which contain mob secrets dating back to the 1920s. It's as if the spirit, or spirits as it seems, of the house were talking to me."

"The ending they foresaw was not pretty — they said the only way they will be free is if the house is destroyed."

"Destroyed, how?"

"By a great calamity. Patrick, I thought this project was a wonderful idea, but now I'm scared."

Patrick was visibly shaken, but he tried to reassure her. "Kitty, you know I would never do anything that would cause harm to you. We'll have to get to the bottom of this murder and the gangster problem. Then perhaps these spirits will be kind to us, as you first thought. Then we can live there in peace."

That night they both slept fitfully, with unsettling visions of the mysterious phenomena they had observed during the day.

Chapter Ten

The next evening was Sunday, and Kitty and Patrick finally planned a quiet evening at home in Mies van der Rohe's classic 860 Lakeshore Drive. As he gazed from their full-wall apartment windows in the fading light of dusk, fog crept in, as a warm front settled over the lake. A foghorn sounded its mournful notes in a fateful dirge. Kitty watched an episode of Murder She Wrote, while Patrick settled in at his roll-top desk. This was the first chance he'd had to spend with the old books he had discovered in the wall safe at the Bond Street house.

When he opened the oldest volume, he was stunned by its contents. He found actual entries by Curly Humphries, Al Capone's behind-the-scenes mastermind. Starting as a wheelman for the gangster's most daring crimes, this bright young recruit showed a talent for working with numbers and strategizing defenses against the government's finest G-men. A legal junkie, he originated the famous Fifth Amendment defense, "I refuse to answer on the grounds that it may tend to incriminate me." His strategies were said to have put off the inevitable defeat of the nationwide mob and, more specifically, the Chicago outfit, by several years.

Patrick fired up his laptop and did some checking on the internet. He found out more about Capone's case and his operations, confirming that Curly Humphries provided the legal and financial backup behind the Capone mob. From his internet research, Patrick had concluded Elliott Ness and his G-men apparently did not have these ledgers at the time of his trial. He wondered if the missing financial records could have been key evidence for him to convict Capone of additional wrongdoing, maybe even including perpetrators of the St. Valentine's Day Massacre. Could they have enabled Ness to get Capone in a stronger conviction and possibly the death penalty for his crimes?

While its appearance at this late date was neither here nor there for the late Capone and his cronies, Patrick began to understand why Candicci was so eager to get them. What better way for Detroit capo Jimmy Romo to blackmail the Chicago mob and gain the upper hand in his takeover attempts? These records held many clues to the location and extent of their operations, even up to the present day.

Patrick was truly thankful that Detective Sergeant O'Malley had vowed to take Candicci out of circulation, postponing another confrontation, while giving Nick and Gloria a chance to establish themselves without the interference of organized crime. It further occurred to him that possession of this information by the FBI might be a scoring opportunity for the law in the court of public opinion—advantage, good guys. At the very least, such evidence had the potential to put an end to the Detroit gang's interference in Gloria and Nick McGurk's fledgling business.

He resolved to have all these documents copied in the morning. Just a block from the old office on Wabash, beneath the elevated tracks, sat the unobtrusive storefront of Certified Blueprint, a document reproduction company run by a loyal confidant. He trusted Paul —he had protected his highly competitive marketing presentations and competition entries over many years. Without even needing to use a courier, he would hand-deliver this precious evidence himself first thing in the morning.

The real challenge, however, would be to get them back in place before Candicci discovered them missing.

The thought was punctuated by the deep tones of the foghorn, "Oo-oo-oooo-GUP..." The plosive second note then cut off sharply, its dying echo accenting the foggy stillness of the lake. Although it no doubt occurred on a fixed interval, the timing felt random — with each repeat it resonated anew, unsettled his gut and immobilized his will.

58

Chapter Eleven

Monday morning Chet joined Patrick by the bank of twenty elevators in the lobby of their new office building. While the lobbies had been upgraded in the mid-thirties with elegant brass tracery on the elevator doors and frames, the cars themselves were the original steel cages, each attended by an operator, with, numerous stops, low speed, and infrequent trips. The delays gave Chet a chance to blurt a barrage of questions. By the time they arrived at the company's floor, he had received a rundown on Kitty's alarming Sunday discoveries at the old house. In the reception area, the sarcastic Yolanda was ready for him. "So Patrick, did you two enjoy your weekend together?"

"We did," Patrick replied, "while you no doubt breakfasted in bed with your secret lover, Kitty and I took a romantic trip into the past."

She snickered and handed Patrick a fistful of While You Were Out messages with one from O'Malley on top. "I think he wants a bite of your ass for breakfast."

"Are you sure you don't?" Patrick said.

"You wish."

They proceeded to Patrick's office and got the detective on his speaker phone.

"MacKenna, it's about time," he said with his usual reproof. "The forensics came back. Fingerprints on the shovel match some we found in the old Detroit hideout up the street. The primary suspects include Marco Candicci, especially because of the—"

"What if it's not Candicci?" Patrick interrupted, without mentioning why, he thought the victim could be someone else.

"Maybe, but Candicci was there, all right. We haven't confirmed the stiff's ID yet. Some of the prints on the shovel handle match his. The blood on the shovel blade matches that of the victim, and it's not Candicci's. We found different prints in another upstairs bedroom. We don't know who else was there."

It was a novel experience to have the detective running down leads for him, but Patrick was enjoying it. He ventured to give him another assignment.

"What if it was one of the home's owners, Hensley Wilson or Charles Simmons? You think you could find something out about them?"

An audible sigh came over the phone. "Did she give any clue to where they are?"

"If the body's not Simmons, she said Wilson left town on assignment as a screenwriter. Somewhere in the Los Angeles area. Maybe Culver City would be a good place to start."

"Based on this evidence, we're going to question Candicci as a person of interest."

"Good luck finding him; you might look first in your own morgue," he wisecracked.

Maybe Kitty was right: what she'd seen was a ghost. Patrick told O'Malley they always heard noises in the old house. But he left out the part about the safe — the bundles of C-notes, the old notebook, ledgers, and hidden passages — and the other clues he was developing. His investigation was a work in progress, he reasoned, justifying his concealment with O'Malley's standard excuse for non-disclosure: nothing was confirmed. He ended the call.

"More leads mean more delays for your house project," Chet said hopefully. "The cops could have the property tied up for months."

This hitch would postpone the time to waive the contract contingency and put up earnest money. From Patrick's savings and a small contribution by Kitty, they had gathered funds to make a non-refundable downpayment of ten percent of the purchase price. But before they did, they had ten days, plus whatever delays the police caused, to modify or get out of the contract.

"Looks like this is going to take a while." Patrick opened the briefcase he had set down on a side chair next to his desk, reached in and pulled out a dark green bottle with a molded glass embossed label, which he handed to Chet. .In the meantime, you and Ellen might enjoy this to make the wait more bearable, Savor it — it's kind of rare,"

"Perfect for Thanksgiving dinner! I won't have to go buy my usual Three Buck Chuck." Chet didn't know much about wine, nor all Patrick's secrets, for which he was thankful. But he was happy to share the spoils of his battles.

Next on his stack of messages, Nick McGurk wanted to talk to him without delay. "You'd better stay in the room for this one," he said, and returned the call.

"Patrick," Nick said, "I'm really feeling pressure from Candicci. Now Jimmy Romo is threatening to come into town and find out what's going on with our casino hotel project. He knows things only you and I know. I can't figure out where he's getting his information."

"Yeah, I found out a few things about that — we need to talk. I need to look at the site excavation work anyway. I'll be out there this afternoon."

Haunted Design

Chapter Twelve

At noon Patrick headed north, ate his bag lunch, turned off the interstate, and turned into the familiar farm access road, now fully prepared with a solid bed of crushed rock and a gravel layer to withstand the frequent trips by dump trucks, construction equipment and trailers. On his left rose the tall slab of the hotel tower, now at its full height and nearing completion. He pulled into the graveled future parking lot, donned his hard hat and met Nick McGurk at the entrance.

Nick greeted him warmly and started the tour of the ground floor lobby and public areas.

"Did you get those last slot machines installed yet?"

"Yes, we're just testing them now." Inside the main door to the lobby, row after row of gaudy illuminated machines lined every aisle and filled every corner. Half a dozen electronics installers stood at the machines, inserting bills, pulling levers and pushing buttons. Nick walked to a console and turned up the room speakers. The typically noisy ring-ring of turning wheels accompanied the room music, which played a repetitive melody to a constant, rapid rhythm. This generated a considerable sense of excitement in the nearly empty hall, reproducing the mood Patrick had seen in such casinos before. He congratulated Nick on creating the stimulating atmosphere generally considered necessary to keep players in a state of frenzy.

They were joined by Rudy Weingard, MacKenna Construction's veteran general superintendent, whom Patrick plied with numerous questions.

"How are the finishes coming along in the guest rooms?" Patrick asked.

"We've almost completed the sixteenth through the twentieth floors." Rudy's voice was raspy, after many years of shouting orders to his men over the roar of construction equipment. "One of these elevators is devoted to serving those rooms only, so we can keep it clean and release the top five floors for occupancy. We're still waiting to finish painting two of the floors and for some Jacuzzis with special fittings to arrive before we can claim them all hundred percent complete."

"We're already using the upper floor suites for dignitaries and special guests," Nick explained.

"Do you have enough painters?"

"We have four and could use a couple more," Rudy said, "but we won't be able to get them until next week."

"Let me show you something. I think you'll be pleased," Rudy said. He pushed the elevator button, and they took the express car. They emerged on the top floor at the Starlight Roof nightclub, a wide-open space surrounded by floor to ceiling window walls. The south third of the roof was an open balcony, with a view in three directions. To the east and south, gentle forested hills surrounded roof tops and steeples of the tiny town of Rockville. To the west, the late afternoon sun glinted off the Rock River, just barely visible in the misty distance below the horizon, as it snaked toward its confluence with the Mississippi, A southwest breeze brought the scent of autumn leaf fires, late blooming flowers and the bracing, crisp smell of the river. Cars crawled along adjacent roads, power launches churned up wakes on the river and a few stalwart sailors guided single-masted sailboats as they tacked slowly upstream or progressed downstream with the current.

"This is amazing! I had hopes but no real idea it would be so nice up here."

"Well done, Patrick," Nick said. "Let's take a closer look inside."

The elevator tower and kitchen were grouped at the center of the roof, but toward the south end of the indoor space, leaving the largest nightclub area on the north side of the building. The center of this large seating and dance floor area was dominated by a twenty-foot diameter clear-domed roof, which afforded a sweeping view of the sky, at this time of day dotted with puffy cumulus clouds.

"At night this will be magical!" Patrick looked out the window toward the north end of the site. They descended back to the ground floor in the elevator. "Let's walk over and look at those creek excavations."

A bucket crane, power shovel, and two bulldozers were occupied widening the creek channel, re-depositing earth to enlarge the central island and placing excess soil into empty dump trucks. which were lined up on the gravel road to haul it away.

Patrick and Nick found the excavating contractor's superintendent checking plans in his trailer.

"Are you balancing of cut and fill?" Patrick asked. "Remember, we have to finish shaping the amphitheater on the south bank and maintain our design elevation for the surface of the island." He pointed out on the contoured site plan the areas where the fill was required.

"We've allowed for that," the superintendent said, "but don't forget, some of that sludge from the river is silt and clay, unsuitable fill material. We're balancing cut and fill, but we'll still have to haul the bad stuff away and bring in more sand, gravel and loam to make surfaces that won't settle but will support ground slabs, structures and good landscaping."

"Sounds like you're on top of it," Patrick said.

◊

Meanwhile, in the living quarters of the farmhouse, Kitty visited with Gloria. Kneeling on the carpet, she rolled a ball back and forth with little Mike. He was named after Patrick's uncle, the contractor who used to be Gloria's employer.

"Patrick and I are so excited about our baby," Kitty said, "we can hardly wait. We're planning to get a room ready."

"Nick is so devoted to Little Mike," Gloria said. "He painted the nursery himself. During the day, he's so glad his office is right upstairs, so he can play with him at lunch time and put him down for his nap."

"He has such pretty eyes, greenish blue. Don't they call that hazel? They sort of look like Uncle Mike's."

"I was hoping for pure blue, like Nick's and mine, but who knows what heredity will decide?" Gloria glanced out the window at the ongoing construction "Do you think you can have your house ready in time?"

"It all depends on the murder investigation, which is dragging out forever. We still can do it if we get control of the house soon."

Gloria led Kitty from the farmhouse across the site on a gravel path to the hotel lobby, where installers were still tinkering with the enormous new slot machines. The visual and acoustic noise of a dozen sound and light displays, accompanied by the piped in excitement music, had reached a deafening pitch. She summoned the crew chief. "Can you take it down about a hundred decibels, so I can explain this place to my friend?"

"Why certainly, ma'am," he said, walked to the control panel and cut the noise to a barely audible background murmur.

"You see, Kitty, my idea of the atmosphere is to tone it down, get rid of this cheap casino feeling. I want to make it more like a sophisticated nightclub and feature music of Frank Sinatra and big band hits of the 50s. This is Pop's dream. It's also what our senior patrons love best. This concept will line up with his plans to book big acts for our concert venue and give the whole place a high-class feeling."

"It's marvelous, Gloria. I can hardly wait to see how it turns out."

"It won't be long now. We're due to open at Thanksgiving, in time for the holidays."

Chapter Thirteen

The next morning Jimmy Romo took the interstate to Rockville and followed the directions Angela Atkins had given him over the phone to the county road. He turned off at the sign, Future Chicago Hotel and Casino Resort and drove his sedan up the winding road and parked in front of the project office in the old farmhouse.

"Angela? Here I am. Is Joe here?"

"He's tied up downtown until this afternoon, I'll let Gloria know you're here." She pressed a button on the intercom and announced his arrival.

"Hi, Uncle Jimmy." Gloria entered and spread her arms in welcome.

"Hi, baby. Wow, look at you! Last time I was here, you were a teenager with braces." He squeezed her in his arms.

"You're looking good for an old guy! Maybe a little tired around the eyes."

Jimmy wasn't really her uncle, but he might as well have been — a second father really, he had always encouraged her. She stood back and looked up at his impressive bulk and height, but his shoulders sagged, his graying hair was mussed, and his long arms hung low to the ground. He'd always reminded her of Bushman, the famous gorilla she'd seen as a child at Lincoln Park Zoo.

"But I just talked to you in Detroit yesterday afternoon," Angela said,

"You drove all night?" Gloria asked.

"It was a long one, all right."

"You must be exhausted, Jimmy. Angie, give him the penthouse suite."

"Thanks, I could use a change of scene." Seated behind her ornate mahogany desk in the upstairs office of the historic farmhouse, she offered Jimmy an opposite wing chair, where he lowered himself with his crossed-legs and leaned forward, his jaw projecting prominently.

"Pop is downtown today, mending fences."

"Looks like the fences out here are in tip-top shape. Who knew you could make this old farm look so classy?"

"You like it? This renovation was my first project in all this." She waved her arm in a proprietary manner toward the whole site.

"What brings you out here? You're usually so careful to stay under the radar."

"It seems I'm the only one who can get what I want." He looked around the room, at the old fireplace, the hearth and Persian rug.

"And you, little pumpkin, you've become such a pretty, sexy young lady. And so smart!"

"Well, Nick thinks so anyway."

"I can't believe you couldn't find any other guy than McGurk as your main squeeze." Romo frowned, his dangling arms made fists, and he looked away.

"Oh, Uncle Jimmy, he's so smart, so clever in business and so good to me — you'll see."

"He's part of my problem. He stole from me, Gloria, as near as we can figure, almost half a million clams — of all the guys out there, why him?"

"Jimmy, he saved my life! You remember that thunderstorm we had at the dedication ceremony for this project? What a mess! He got me out of there and almost saved me, but your goons took advantage of the confusion and kidnapped me. They held me prisoner for weeks, until Nick and Patrick figured out where he rescued me—again."

"I was in Miami. I didn't realize — good for him, and for you! "

"He's my hero,"

"I guess I'm better off with him running a private business than messing up our operations. I'll grant you, he's clever and smart about money."

"Then why didn't you promote him, give him some encouragement?"

"It's a big organization — these things take time. He was impatient, and the way he got out — all the money he stole. I'll never forgive him now."

"Please do me a favor and consider it a loan. He had to get started somehow, and he's just not up for the Outfit. We're good for it here, we'll make payments — even cover the vig. This operation has made money from day one."

"Pumpkin, you know I'd do anything for you. But business is business. You can forget the vig. Just return the principal and make me whole again."

"Oh, thank you, Jimmy. I love him so much. Wait until you meet our baby boy!"

Romo stood and took a turn around the parlor, pounding his head in simian fashion. The strain on the aging mobster caught up with him and coaxed him back to his chair.

"That boy Marco is practically worthless, and I'm here to straighten him out."

"Jimmy, why don't you quit? You sure don't need the money. You deserve some me-time after all your hard work."

"You know we can't retire from this business. You're lucky you've got me to deal with me in Detroit and not some young buck. I've had a good enough life. It's up to the new generation now.

"But it's been done before, Jimmy. There's that capo from Long Island that did his time and quit — what was his name — Franceze?"

"Oh, yeah, the holy roller, running around the country claiming he's found God. No thanks. Once some new wise guy takes over, I'll be leaving all right, but feet first."

Gloria looked out the window of the office at scudding cumulus clouds, mostly blocking the sun. Tears filled her eyes over Jimmy's fate, Still, she had to look ahead, to her future. As she watched, the racing clouds parted. A ray of sun brightened the room and lit a colorful diamond on the carpet. She had everything to live for. If he wanted to turn things over to a new generation, she was ready.

"Pop wants to leave something behind for me to keep — something I can work toward and build."

"I'm rough on Marco. Maybe he'll shape up before Joe goes away. I was hoping you and he could take over here. Now look at him — a murder suspect, not even smart enough to stay out of trouble."

"That's why Nick got out. He hates all the robbing and killing, struggling to reach the top and fighting to stay there. He's too smart for that."

Romo paced over to the window and soaked up the direct sunlight, "Feels good, soothes these aching bones." When he turned back toward Gloria, his dark eyes no longer glowered, but glittered, his face more relaxed.

"Pop wants me to have my dream: Nick and I can own this business free and clear, give folks a straight deal — raise a family in peace live out our lives and retire."

"Yeah," Marco said." Too late for Joe and me, but there's a chance for you kids."

She felt the ground shifting beneath her. The clouds were gone, and one huge weight was lifted from her, while she shouldered another. Yet the burden seemed light. She and Nick were learning how to run this large enterprise. Jimmy sighed and held her as if his life depended on it. "Punkin, I just want the best for you."

"Then Jimmy, let Nick and me alone and let us run our business."

Uncle Jimmy, who had guided her through troubled times growing up, now needed her. It was her turn to lead, and she took a deep breath. "You can catch Pops later, when he gets back from the city."

"In case I don't see you before you leave—" The thought brought tears to her eyes, and she probed deep into her father's lore for something to fill the void. She quoted Joe's old Irish blessing, "May you get to Heaven half an hour before the devil knows you're dead!"

"Ha," Jimmy said, and shook his head, "too bad I'm not Irish. I doubt if it will apply."

Much as she loved him, she wondered what unfinished business had really brought him here. It was unlikely to help the project. Some might call it the devil's work.

Chapter Fourteen

Back downtown later that afternoon, Patrick called Chet in and closed the door to his office. He picked up the phone and pressed the receptionist's button. "Yolanda, hold my calls for the next half hour, please.

"Chet, things are moving too fast. For once I have an extremely uneasy feeling about having Chicago Joe as our client."

"I don't want to say I told you so, but I have worried about this since the start of this project. I've been relying on your confidence you can work for Joe, weed out the bad guys, and still do our project. So far you've been right. At this late date, what's the problem?"

"I'm losing confidence in law enforcement itself. We're all naturalized citizens in my family, and I've always been prouder than a native son that I can call myself an American. With this latest election, our country could be changed beyond recognition. It's not just the top office, either. At the state and local levels they all lie about established facts, and gullible folks — apparently lots of them — believe them. The changes they want in government are appalling. They all talk lik mob bosses and even behave like them."

"Some days I lose heart myself. Even Joe is ashamed he got his start in the gangs. He wishes he could get out of the mob."

"He won't be able to quit. Nastier bosses will force people like Joe out. With politics like they've been lately, law enforcement will grind to a halt. I don't know what I'll do."

"I hate to think what could happen to this project," Chet added"people like Candicci and the South Side gang will take over and force Gloria and Nick out. We lose a good client and they lose their chance for a new start."

"I feel like I'm sinking in quicksand. We try to buy a house and there's a body in it. We try to fix it up and there are people crawling around it trying to chase us out. Maybe I don't believe in spirits, but I do know when somebody's out to get me. When I think how hard we've worked to get where we are and how far we could fall, I get scared."

Chet had seldom seen Patrick like this. He was losing his bearings and doubting his own instincts, which up to now had been flawless and dependable. He had to do something fast.

"Look Patrick," he said, "get hold of yourself. Let's work on those things we can control."

"Like what?"

"In the meantime, nothing has changed. We have a great project for a good client, the police and the FBI have a murder case to solve, and we'll help if we can.

"Joe is no ordinary mobster," Chet went on. "He works hard to make sure his daughter Gloria and Nick will have a fresh start in life. He cares about people, loves music, and puts his family before everything and everyone. Let's forget our misgivings and move on."

"Gotta hand it to you, Chet, it's all we can do."

If Chet had any inkling of what lay ahead, he would have eaten his words.

Chapter Fifteen

Candicci returned to the Bond Street property late on Sunday morning, He removed a brick in the back wall of the house, inserted a large skeleton key into an old-fashioned rim lock and swung open a heavy door faced with brick matching the exterior wall. He entered and swung the door closed from inside. A sunbeam from a high window in the stair tower illuminated the passage and lit up motes of dust swirling at the disturbance of his entry.

Climbing to the second floor, he entered the master bedroom. The temporary drafting table in the window had been cleared of architect's tools and the drawing pad. The Tiffany lamp, a dirty doily and a cut glass candy dish were the only objects still in original positions on the antique tabletop. He shed his suit coat and cap, laid them on the four-poster bed, and went to work. He removed the oil portrait of the ancestor from the wall at the bedside, dialed the familiar combination and swung open the door to the safe. Shining his powerful flashlight into the void, he grabbed his spray can on the top shelf and lubricated the heavy hinges from inside. Directing the beam to the middle shelf, he checked the neatly stacked piles of cash for the number of packets in each and found them undisturbed. But the lower shelf was empty — the two canvas bound account ledgers and the school notebook with the splattered cover design were gone.

"Mother of Satan!" He surprised himself with this utterance. Italian curse words no longer came easily to his tongue — he'd been consorting with Irish crooks for too long. He'd picked up their expressions, and he didn't even get them right.

Trembling, he reclosed the safe, restored the portrait to its place, donned his jacket and hat and climbed to his attic warren. He pulled a fresh pack of unfiltered Chesterfields from his suit jacket, lit one and began pacing in a tight circle around the small attic room. Calmed by this nervous activity, he settled into his wing chair. With trembling fingers he lit a new smoke with the tip of his first and settled in to wait. The close air from the room, built-up smoke and his new predicament caused him to sweat furiously and toss his jacket and hat on the facing wing chair. What would Jimmy Romo say — in fact, what would he do? His panic increased as he faced the inevitability of confronting him. He pondered his predicament: how could he deal with these intrusive occupants? When it was vacant he had the run of it. He sat immobile for a long time until, still sitting upright and clueless, he dozed off.

He awoke with a start when his cell phone rang, He stared at it blankly until the fog cleared and he recalled where he was.

He grabbed the phone and answered the call.

"Marco?" A familiar, brash voice snapped him to attention.

"Hey Jimmy, it's you! How come no sound effects? "

"Because I'm right here in town, Marco. It seems when I leave matters to you everything gets screwed up."

"What's wrong?"

"You've got a problem, Marco, The old ledgers and the notebook — they're missing from the safe. Have you got them?"

Damn! Busted, before he had a chance to explain.

"Yeah, I know. I just checked."

"Where did they go?"

His mind raced, but nothing came out.

"You sure you didn't take them yourself?"

"I swear on my mother's grave I don't have them. It's those new buyers, over there meddling all the time. But I have a plan to get them back — you'll have them within a week."

"You'd better, or you'll be lying right next to your mother in that cemetery — if they ever find you, that is." He ended the call.

He sat in his wing chair, sweating, grasping for that plan he'd promised Jimmy. He didn't know how long he'd been puzzling over it when he heard a man's and a woman's voice on the floor below, then footsteps on the main stairway. His eyes darting in all directions, he waited quietly to see what would happen. Then an idea dawned on him — a solution to all his problems.

◊

While Candicci made his excuses with Jimmy Romo that morning on how and why he had lost control of the ledgers, Patrick and Kitty followed their leisurely Sunday morning routine at their lakeside apartment. He mentioned that he and Chet had finished their measurements. A draftsman at the office had completed floor plans for the basement and the three living levels in of the house, showing all the hidden passages and rooms.

"Good. It will make our planning easier. I can't wait to get in there again and evaluate my room plans against the actual floor plan."

"With these gangsters on the loose, it's not safe for you to work in the house alone anymore. Although there's a warrant out for him, the police haven't found Marco Candicci."

"I can help solve this problem," Kitty kept talking, ignoring the Patrick's point. "I understand these spirits and can figure out what they're doing," she insisted.

"No, it's too dangerous! These intruders are real. And we know they are members of the mob."

"I have a clear conscience, and I fear no evil spirits that ever smelled o' brimstone."

"Oh, that's not what I'm talking about!" Patrick steamed in frustration. "Let's spend the night there, together. I'll bring my gun."

"I doubt it will help against the spirits — they're already dead."

"Just in case one of them happens to be flesh and blood."

◊

To avoid leaving an obvious clue, that afternoon Patrick and Kitty took a cab to the house property. They also took Buster: they couldn't bear to leave him alone in that barren, lonely apartment. Settled in the house by nightfall, they made the bed, lay down with their clothes on, turned out the lights and chatted in the dark. Buster snuggled into the bed next to Kitty. They were both fully clothed except for shoes, loosely covered by the owners' quilted duvet, in the event they had to contend with night prowlers.

Restless at first, Patrick sat upright on the bed and scanned the room for clues. The bookcase sat opposite the foot of the bed, with aging, leather-bound volumes of some classic nineteenth century writers. The alcove with the writing desk was beyond Kitty on his left. He absentmindedly explored the nightstand with his right hand, found a handle, and opened the drawer. He withdrew an envelope with a US stamp and a New York postmark addressed to Charles Simpson at the address of this house. Guiltily he withdrew a few pages of handwritten text on onionskin paper. Overruling privacy considerations and the niceties of social etiquette, he justified this snooping on grounds that any clue to the   relationship of these two residents could help solve the murder case.

Dearest Charlie,

> *After preparing the final draft of the introduction*
> *for my live, televised interview tomorrow of the*
> *"Great Author," I figured there was nothing more*
> *to say, since his rabid fans would beat the doors*
> *down just to hear him anyway, and I was done. It*
> *was only dinnertime, so I ate a burger and fries*
> *across the street from the theater and pounced on*
> *the box office exactly a half-hour before showtime.*
> *I scored an unclaimed orchestra seat for that*
> *musical I've been wanting to see. It was a bad*
> *show, but the excitement of being in the theater,*
> *the music, the lights and the performers singing*
> *their hearts out made me feel like a kid again ...*

The letter continued to describe his excitement, absorbed like a youngster again in the darkened theater, without being watched or judged by anyone else with whispered comments, like, "Why does that gay guy come to a straight show like this?" When the lights came up after the final curtain, he sat weeping in his seat. The lady sitting next to him said, "You poor dear, I don't know what's wrong, but I'm so sorry." She hugged him.

The letter went on, but Patrick had read enough. These guys really had something, and it was sad that they could no longer carry on the house project together. He carefully put the letter back in its envelope and returned it to the drawer.

Kitty lay on the bed, her eyes closed. Patrick fell asleep beside her when his head hit the pillow. Scenes from Abigail's ghost stories raced through her mind — the serving maid, the jealous cook, her cheating husband. Sleep would not come. She kept her eyes closed, listening, alert for their presence.

A loud plop on the floor startled her. She sat up, cast the duvet aside, and slipped into her shoes. In the dim light through a crack in the curtains she spotted a large black box on the floor. The bookcase opposite the bed had an empty space on the top shelf. She restored the boxed book to its slot and turned back toward the bed. Before she could climb in, the book fell again. She stared in wonder. True, the book was so wide it overhung the narrow shelf by a bit, but she was quite sure she had pushed it all the way in. Accustomed to supernatural signs from her childhood in Ireland, though, she sensed what this meant. The spirits of the house were trying to tell her something.

She picked it up, sat on the bed and lit a small lamp on the bedside table. The box had a printed cover glued to its face, entitled: "Tales of Mystery and Imagination." A handsome tinted ink drawing graced the page. In the stylized image faded by age, a crowned King embraced a tall, elaborately draped woman. Behind her, facing to one side, stood a line of similarly clad attendants. The last servant in line held the trailing garment of a woman who seemingly was first in an endless queue of variously clad characters, waiting for an audience with the royal personage. The gray-faced monarch confided in his queen with a sober expression, as if to advise her of the emotional, desperate stories about to come forth from his anxious petitioners. Beneath the drawing was the line: "with illustrations by Harry Clarke." The next line identified the author: Edgar Allen Poe

Kitty's convent school in Ireland had urged pupils to read widely. However, most of the nuns discouraged reading such frivolous genres as novels, murder mysteries, and horror tales such as those of Poe. They considered them an unnecessary distraction from the proper preparation of the young woman of today. Her English teacher, Mother O'Brien, confessed to her senior students, though, that she enjoyed them. She even assigned some of Poe's stories for reading in the class. That was all Kitty and her friends needed. During their summer holidays they read and traded copies of adventure stories, mysteries, and ghost stories, especially those with spiritual elements, in true Irish tradition. She had read Poe's most famous stories and was fascinated to discover this rare volume.

She carefully lifted the cover of the box. It contained a heavy cloth-bound volume with sturdy black cover boards and endpapers. On the front a yellowed white sticker bore a black ink drawing of a kneeling lover beseeching his mistress and repeated the same title information as the image as on the box. She opened it carefully, with the respect due such a treasure. The scent of old paper and ink greeted her from the yellowed pages of this very old special edition, dated MCMXXXIII, from The Tudor Press, New York The Table of Contents confirmed this was an anthology of Poe's most celebrated tales — Ligeia, The Pit and the Pendulum, The Tell-Tale Heart, and The Murders in the Rue Morgue. These and the other stories included in the volume had established him as the originator of the horror story, if not the entire mystery genre. A red satin ribbon trailing from the spine bookmarked the unforgettable fable, The Tell-Tale Heart. It had been years since she had first read it. Kitty opened the book to that story and began to read.

It opened with the testimony of a dreadfully nervous man endowed with acute hearing and broad perception, who lives in a large mansion with an older host. Her eyes fastened on one passage on the first page:

> How, then, am I mad? Hearken! and observe how calmly
> I can tell you the whole story.

> It is impossible to say how first the idea entered my
> brain; at once conceived, it haunted me day and night.
> Passion there was none. I loved the old man. He had
> never wronged me. He had never given the insult. For his
> gold I had no desire. I think it was his eye! Yes, it was
> that! He had the eye of a vulture — a pale blue, with a
> film over it. Whenever it fell upon me, my blood ran

cold; and so by degrees — very gradually — I made up my mind to take the life of the old man, and thus rid myself of the eye forever.

Now this is the point. Mad men know nothing, but you should have seen me. You should have seen how wisely I proceeded — with what caution — with what foresight — with what dissimulation I went to work! I was never kinder to the old man than during the whole week before I killed him.

Patrick still dozed peacefully, but Kitty's mind was astir. She was tempted to wake him and get his opinion of what this incident might mean. What spirit presented this tale to her? Who was trying to tell her something, and why? But she doubted she would take her concerns seriously.

She read until her eyelids were heavy and fell asleep. When she awoke, she heard thumping and rattling sounds. Aware from the progress of moonlight across the carpet that some time had passed, she found the open book beside her on the bed. She tossed the boxed volume into the backpack she had brought along for her camera and binder of notes on improvements. She slipped the backpack over her shoulders in case they decided to leave in a hurry.

The noises that had disturbed her sleep continued. Buster shook off the covers, stood on the bed and perked up his ears. She alerted Patrick and he climbed out of bed. He stealthily sprang open a closet door and shined his powerful light within. Except for cobwebs, sprinkled plaster crumbs and an accumulation of dust, there was nothing in the small enclosure. Even a shelf and pole for hanging clothes held nothing. Kitty followed him in and listened intently. Bumping noises and a low moan reached their ears.

"You stay in the bedroom," Patrick called out, "keep your cell phone on, and I'll make the rounds. Let me know if you hear anything."

Patrick slid aside a false back wall in the closet, which he had found on his last visit, poked his head through, and looked up and down the stairs of the tower. He neither heard nor saw anything. He retreated, took the main stairway, and descended to check all the floors and doors from basement to attic in the house.

Kitty was far too independent and curious — a trait she shared with Patrick — to sit trembling in the bedroom for her presumed "safety." She was a sitting duck no matter where she remained. It would be better, she figured, to stay in motion and find the intruders, whether human or ghost, and confront them directly, gaining the element of surprise — an intemperate decision she might regret, but she was worried enough to risk it.

She climbed to the third floor, where it was very dark and smoky. The dim rays of a streetlight penetrated a narrow crack between thick velvet curtains. unnoticed and protective, Buster trailed behind her.

As her eyes adjusted to the gloom, through the smoke appeared the vague outline of a large male form. She recognized the specter she had seen before and gasped. Silently cursing her error, she froze. Even the dog, disoriented, stared soundless into the void.

The figure turned and faced in her direction. She made out the shadowy shape of a tall, muscular man, leaning toward her. Her heart pounding, she spoke, resolved to confront the vague specter. "Oh spirit—"

"It's you, again. little one," A rough voice growled. "Just in time. You come with me, or I'll fix you, forever!"

She retreated toward the closet where she had entered the room.

Now the darkness was total and took on a different quality. The smoke parted and the air cleared. She now was overtaken by a tingling sensation and couldn't move her legs. She felt her will leaving her, at a rare loss for words. If this was a ghost, it was a powerful one.

Her heart pounded, yet she still could not move. In a dreamlike state, she saw a new vision: this specter was the embodiment of a word that silently appeared in a cloud — E-V-I-L!

Chapter Sixteen

Buster burst into a frenzy of barking, interspersed with angry growls. Kitty's bravado evaporated into the darkness. She screamed and turned to retreat through the hidden stairwell but. paralyzed with fear, was rooted to the spot. One cold hand grabbed her by an arm, the other encircled her waist and cast her face down on the scatter rug. She realized too late he was not an immaterial figment, but real flesh and blood. Gasping to catch her breath, she got a nose full of dust, moldy air, and smoke and sneezed violently.

"Kitty, where are you?" Patrick's voice echoed up the tower stairs, along with the sound of him clambering up to the third level. Removing the Glock from his pants pocket, he reached the hidden door to the back bedroom.

Overpowered, too breathless for a word of reply, she resisted, squealed, and squirmed for advantage. The huge figure hoisted Kitty over his shoulder, her legs flailing in front of him. He was halfway down the front stairway by the time Patrick entered the attic.

In the dim glow from the crack in the curtain, Patrick leveled his pistol into the shadows. "Freeze!" he yelled.

Silence, except for distant thumping.

He searched the wall with his left hand for the light switch and flicked it on. Everywhere were signs of a scuffle: disordered furniture and a displaced rug, but no trace of Kitty. He followed the sounds to the main staircase, where she had dropped one of her barrettes as a clue to their route. He crept down a flight, his pistol pointed forward and found the other barrette on the second-floor landing. Across the master bedroom, at the open door to the hidden stairway, lay a crumpled tissue, no doubt the last item Kitty possessed to mark her trail. He entered the tower stairwell, felt a blast of cool air below, and descended toward the exit. At the ground floor, he found the source of the draft — opposite the door from the vestibule the concealed panel hung open to the driveway. He raced through the opening toward the street, too late. An engine roared and a pair of taillights retreated a half block away.

"Dammit!" Patrick muttered. He grabbed his cell phone and called O'Malley on speed dial. He heard some fumbling noises then a grunt in response. "O'Malley, wake up!"

"For chrissake, Patrick. It's the middle of the night — Sunday night, by the way."

"Shut up and get this! I'm at this house property, and a mobster has just made off with Kitty."

"Oh, crap. Who was it?"

"I just got a glimpse of him running down the stairs with Kitty over his shoulder kicking and screaming. He's tall, but who knows?

"Where did they go?"

"It's a powerful car, dark color, headed north on Bond Street."

"Oh, that narrows it down considerably." The detective was fully awake now, restored to his sarcastic, disagreeable self.

"Dammit, O'Malley, none of your wisecracks. It's all I've got — and it's the most important case of your life!"

"I'm on it, you son of a bitch," the detective groused. "You'll have a squad car there in ten minutes. I haven't slept in three days. Good night!" The line went dead.

Patrick turned and looked for the dog, who had been right on Kitty's heels. "Oh my god1" he exclaimed, "Buster jumped into the car!"

This thought was his only comfort in the catastrophe. He re-entered the tower, swung the heavy, brick-clad door closed and climbed to the bedroom alcove to wait.

86

Chapter Seventeen

After arriving back at the apartment at two a.m. Patrick slept a fitful three hours. A ding on his phone woke him at five — an "URGENT" text summoned him. He dragged his exhausted frame out of bed, put on his clothes from a heap on the chair, and jammed his stocking feet into his loafers. With a herculean effort, almost sleepwalking, he shuffled to the kitchen for coffee.

Promptly at eight he entered the Chicago FBI office, where Agent Radwinski was waiting for him. Atypically, O'Malley was already there.

"Morning Radi," Patrick said. "Detective. I see you recovered from your sleep deprivation. What's so much more urgent than last night's disaster?"

"Homeowner Hensley Wilson just got into town," O'Malley informed him. "We're ready to start interviewing him and thought you might like to sit in."

"From the tone of the message I thought somebody died."

"Somebody did," the FBI agent reminded him. "We think we know who."

"Abigail will have a fit when she learns I'm meeting directly with the other seller without her present."

"Forget her blasted real estate ethics." Radwinski said. "We're talking murder here."

The news that the death was no longer considered accidental, at least, sounded like progress in the law's slow walk to justice.

The three entered the conference room, O'Malley made the introductions, read Wilson his rights and stated that the interview would be recorded on video.

Hensley Wilson was of medium height, with a small frame, blond hair, and expressive blue eyes that looked pleadingly at the group.

"How did it happen that a body was found in the coal bin of the house?" O'Malley began.

"As I mentioned on the phone, I don't know. I haven't been living there. When I was hired to write a screenplay for a Hollywood producer, I moved to California. We decided to sell the house. We'd given up on the restoration, and Charles planned to stay until we sold the property."

"We viewed the body at the morgue yesterday," O'Malley said, glancing toward the video camera in the ceiling corner. "Tell us what you found."

"It was Charlie, all right. Same black hair, high cheekbones, strong physique, and…" He broke off, sobbing.

"I'm sorry for your loss, Mr. Wilson. "So, you are positively identifying the victim as co-owner Charles Simmons, who was staying in the house at the time?" Radwinski said.

"Yes."

"According to our lab reports," O'Malley added. "His blood type and DNA matched the blood on the shovel blade."

"So, based on the fingerprints on the grip handle, the killer was Candicci," Patrick said, "Right?"

"Guess again," Agent Radwinski said. "The few prints on the wooden handle were indistinct, and the metal hasp connecting the blade to the wood handle had no prints, probably wiped clean. We're back to square one on who that was."

"What about the blood on it. Did you check the DNA?" Patrick said.

"The blood was the victim's, but we can't prove how it got there nor who the perp was. Do you have anything to add, Mr. Wilson?"

"Apparently Charlie surprised somebody when he was checking the coal bin — before our first winter coal delivery arrived. Poor Charlie!"

The interview was effectively over. Wilson voluntarily left a blood sample and a set of fingerprints. He was overcome with grief. Radwinski, despite his cool office demeanor, took pity on him, unwilling to prolong his suffering.

Chapter Eighteen

O'Malley paid a visit to the architectural office the next morning. Sheepish, he asked for Patrick, and Yolanda escorted him into the conference room. She reappeared with his customary drink — coffee-flavored, sugared milk.

"I sure prefer to come over here. At our office. I'm constantly interrupted, the coffee stinks, and the place is still infested with wildlife." He reached up and scratched an itch on his shoulder. They still hadn't cured the persistent bedbug problem at police headquarters.

"Any time, Detective. I'm terrified for Kitty. She can't withstand any rough treatment, Our future depends on finding her soon." She's pregnant with our first child.

"No wonder you're so upset."

"Well, yeah. Wouldn't you be?"

"Maybe I was a bit short with you — I'm so sleep deprived I was glued to the bed. Here's a copy of the report my officers made at your prospective house Sunday night."

"They came right away and scoured the place, although this guy was a real pro and left very few clues. I'll be interested to see any other prints or DNA they find."

"They examined the safe," O'Malley said. "They couldn't open it. But the forensic team lifted some new fingerprints. They match Candicci's. Look out for a ransom note."

"Great." Patrick shifted in his chair and changed the subject. "I told the officers about the house up the street. Did they find anything there?"

"Our officers found it locked up tight. They inspected the premises, tried all the doors and looked through all the windows. There were no lights inside. As nearly as they could determine the house was unoccupied."

◊

After the meeting Patrick returned to his desk and called Nick McGurk.

"Nick, we've got problems. Kitty's been kidnapped. I suspect it's Candicci."

"Oh my God! What happened?"

"He's entering our future house and causing trouble — he may think it will disrupt our casino plans." He related the events of the previous evening and Kitty's terrifying capture.

"There's no way they would try to hide her a few doors away," Nick said.

"Yeah, when he roared away in that car, I figured he wasn't stopping for anything, certainly not on the same street. The police report is useless."

"Still, before he grabbed her, he might have been living in the gang hideout up the street. What can I do to help?"

"What if we revive our covert surveillance team? We need to conduct a fact-finding tour of my prospective neighborhood."

"I'm game. When?"

"Why don't we start tonight? Bring your burglar tools."

Patrick and Nick had worked together like this before. When Gloria was held hostage in the gang hideout up the street, the cops were clueless. The two teamed up to free her and capture the crooks.

In the evening at about ten o'clock Patrick, dressed in his dark prowling clothes, met Nick McGurk at the Detroit gang's old hideout up the street from their future home. The windows were dark. They knocked on the front door and no one answered. Since this operation was highly illegal, they approached unobtrusively from the basement entry. Besides, it was easier: Nick produced a skeleton key that fit the old rim lock and then jimmied the cylinder lock. Fortunately, there was no chain.

"Let's slip on our gloves," Patrick said. "We don't want to disturb the evidence any more than necessary — and especially not leave any."

They entered the hideout through the damp, mold-infested basement and stealthily made their way upstairs. The deserted house appeared as if someone had left in a hurry. In the kitchen, they found coffee cups in the sink and a pile of dirty plates. Patrick had brought plastic bags and a canvas tote bag to hold evidence. He selected a few cups, plates, and utensils. Upstairs he added a drinking glass from the bathroom and a polished wood coat hanger from the closet in the main bedroom. Two six-hundred-dollar suits hung on the rod. On the top shelf he found Candicci's fedora, with its signature red feather in the band. He might as well leave a clue to give the police something to do.

Next, he searched the second bedroom.

"Whoa! Look what we have in here," Patrick said. The bed was unmade, dirty underwear stowed in a plastic bag. A pair of pants and a jacket, not nearly so costly as Candicci's, hung on the rod, and a pair of size ten shoes cluttered the floor of the closet. Dresser drawers were empty but one was open. In the wastebasket, Patrick found a crumpled note with a couple of phone numbers on a sheet taken from the printed pad of a savings-and-loan company, which he slipped into the pocket of his windbreaker for future reference.

"Whew," Nick whistled. "Somebody left here fast — and he forgot to check the closet."

"There's no doubt Candicci and somebody else have been camping here. I'll have O'Malley send a CSI team over here to collect more evidence. We've done all we can do here tonight."

"Right, let's pack it in."

By the time they had finished their surveillance and collection, it was getting close to midnight. Patrick put his few souvenirs in the back of his Honda, Nick hopped into his Mustang, and they took off for their separate homes.

Part II: Haunted Hearts

When I had made an end of these labors, it was four o'clock — still dark as midnight. As the bell sounded the hour, there came a knocking at the street door. I went down to open it with a light heart — for what one had I now to fear? There entered three men, who introduced themselves, with perfect suavity, as officers of the police. A shriek had been heard by a neighbor during the night, suspicion of foul play had been aroused, information had been lodged in the police office, and they (the officers) had been deputed to search the premises.I

I smiled — for what had I to fear? I bade the gentlemen welcome.

—Edgar Allen Poe, "The Telltale Heart," 1843

—

Chapter Nineteen

The kidnapper burst out of the hidden door in the side wall of the tower, thrust his burden face down through the rear car door, which he had left open, and bound Kitty's wrists. He opened the rear door. When he faced forward to close it, Buster leaped into the rear seat. The kidnapper got in, set the child lock on his late-model Mustang, and pulled away.

Buster curled up in her lap and remained quiet but alert.

"You — you idjut!" Kitty exclaimed. "You'll never get away with this. And untie me. This hurts."

"You be quiet, or I'll shut you up myself, and that will hurt more."

With no choice, she was reduced to muttering curses under her breath. Lulled by the hypnotic drone of the powerful engine, the swish of traffic, and the extreme darkness of the car's interior, she stroked Buster's fur until she fell asleep.

He turned north and zigzagged until he got to a main artery, crossed the river, and headed for the interstate, northbound. At this hour inbound trucks cruised in the opposite lanes, but few vehicles impeded progress in his direction. He proceeded at the speed limit — a traffic stop now would be disastrous. He had to reach his destination uninterrupted.

He checked the back seat in the rearview. His captive slumped against the door in the dark, exhausted from struggle.

As he settled into cruise mode, his mind raced back over his frantic flight from the city over the past week. Packing some of his clothes and essentials from the Bond Street hideout, he had hunted for a safe place to escape Romo's detection. He scoured the North Shore until he reached the main street of Ridgewood, a small Italian settlement a few stops up the lakefront from Winnetka, Highland Park and the other, better-known bedroom communities. He'd found a vacant furnished flat over the shops on Main Street, large enough to accommodate a guest, originally built for the shop owner's family. His business style of dress and habits would attract less attention, and he could lay low, hidden from Romo's crew until he could produce enough results to satisfy Jimmy. His only salvation would be to produce the missing financial ledgers and daily journals, the object of Romo's rage, so critical to the latter-day outfit's survival.

Jumpy on his nicotine high, he checked his passenger, now dozing on her side across the rear seat. She had a hotter temper than most females he'd met. He wasn't looking forward to dealing with her when she woke up.

Forty minutes later he slid into the parking slot behind his rental flat and stretched his legs, taking in the crisp, early morning air. His watch showed 2:15 a.m.

His prisoner still lay cramped on the seat. He lifted her out and climbed the stairs of the back porch, hidden by darkness from the oblivious, sleeping town.

The dog jumped out, barked furiously, and followed them up the steps.

"Crap! Who let that mutt in there?"

"You did'" Kitty said, awakened by the movement and the dog's racket, "Buster looks out for me."

He carried her inside, dumped her on the bed in the spare bedroom and returned to the kitchen. He fixed a plate with a fried chicken leg, a slice of bread and a can of ginger ale from the fridge and set them on the bedside table. He left a water dish and some table scraps for the dog on the floor. Now fully awake, Kitty leaned on one elbow and squinted her eyes open.

"Where have you taken me, you bastard?" she demanded.

"It will be nice and safe here, hidden from the mob and everyone else."

"Wh—." Her rage delayed speech, but only for a moment. "Why are you doing this? What do you want? Why me?" She fired her questions with machine-gun rapidity.

"Here, let me make you more comfortable." The dog growled as he pulled a switch blade from his pocket and opened it.

She stared wide-eyed as he cut the tape binding her wrists.

"I need to make a deal with that meddler MacKenna. This is the best way to get his attention."

"You'll get it all right," she said, "and you'll be sorry!"

"Calm down, babe. We're going to be very happy here."

"Don't call me babe — I'm a fully grown woman and you won't be happy to know me."

Candicci sighed. "It's the middle of the night. I'm going to let you get to sleep. Here's food if you're hungry, and the john is right over there." He set down a plate and turned to leave the room.

"You- you worm! I'll rip ye apart with my bare hands."

Candicci left the room and locked the door from the outside with a sickening click.

Chapter Twenty

The nighttime fog was gone, and rosy dawn tinted the indigo sky. The bright sun — restoring not only light but growth, hope, and a fresh new day for humankind — cast generous rays on the tiny town. On church stained-glass and cracking, dirty window it shined alike; on gleaming tower and rotting wall it spread its healing light. It lit up the room where Kitty lay with her loyal cockapoo. Though her capture had been grim in that fog-bound predawn hour, what might brilliant light of day portend?

Kitty opened her eyes wide and took stock of her newfound plight. She scoured her pockets for her cell phone but recalled she had left it at the old house, charging in the window alcove.

On this bedside table, cleared of chicken bones and the empty can from her midnight snack, now sat a plate with half an orange, a doughnut, and a cup of watery coffee. Her flesh crawled to think this serpent had slithered in as she slept to leave this prison fare — the nerve of this cruel monster! She had no other choice but to eat. The orange was overripe, the doughnut stale and the coffee sour and bitter. Rage rose anew in her heaving chest.

In describing his work, Patrick had explained what he did in such situations. A captured soldier's first duty, he'd once explained, is to escape. But she had little heart nor strength for such a daring feat. In the light of day, she saw she'd gotten it wrong. The key to her release was right before her eyes,

She'd walked into this hot mess trying to learn more about these crooks. Why stop now? This was her opportunity — she had her prey where she wanted. He couldn't leave either: instead of sneaking around undetected as before, she could study him at close range. Now she could pick his brain. With a little luck she could use him for her own ends. It's much safer, she thought, to keep this heartless hothead cool. With all this time, she'd beat him at his game.

Why had Candicci had never paid for his misdeeds? Patrick said that every time he was questioned by police, he had an alibi and chatted with them in a relaxed and natural manner. She thought of Poe's short story. She grabbed it from her backpack and flipped to the page:

> If you still think me mad, you will think so no longer when I describe the wise precautions I took for the concealment of the body. The night waned, and I worked hastily, but in silence. First of all I dismembered the corpse. I cut off the head and the arms and legs.
>
> I then took three planks on the flooring of the chamber, and deposited all between the scantlings. I then replaced the boards so cleverly, so cunningly, that no human eye — not even his — could have detected any thing wrong. There was nothing to wash out — no stain of any kind — no blood spot whatever. I had been too wary for that. A tub had caught all — ha! ha!
>
> When I had made an end of these labors, it was four o'clock — still dark as midnight. As the bell sounded the hour, there came a knocking at the street door. I went down to open it with a light heart — for what one had I now to fear? There entered three men, who introduced themselves, with perfect suavity, as officers of the police. A shriek had been heard by a neighbor during the night, suspicion of foul play had been aroused, information had been lodged in the police office, and they (the officers) had been deputed to search the premises.
>
> I smiled — for what had I to fear? I bade the gentlemen welcome.

He gives them a tour of the house, demonstrates that the old man's treasures are secure and finally leads them to the bedroom. He arranges chairs for them and sits over the very spot where the corpse is concealed. They chat about ordinary things for a long time. He begins to get annoyed when they do not leave. He babbles away until he develops a severe headache. He then hears the muffled beating of his victim's heart, but the officers do not. He becomes more and more disturbed by these phenomena, until at last he confesses his foul deed.

She wondered if, like the subject of the story, she got him talking and listened long enough, he might lead her directly to what made him tick.

Candicci himself was not a ghost, but a sorry excuse for a human being. He'd shown his true nature — a bundle of evil intent. He was not to be trusted, believed or relied upon for anything. Among the other truths Patrick had shared with Kitty, he had explained the mob and their methods, what they had done to Chicago, and in fact to this young nation of America.

While these dark thoughts occupied her, the sun on this beautiful day had risen high in the sky. Her ravenous hunger reminded her of her miserable breakfast. As part of her campaign to turn the tables on her captor, she would have to do something about adequate meals. She made full use of the limited facilities to clean herself up with the only soap and towel available and formed her plan.

Eventually her captor unlocked the door to her tiny room. He peered around the door, his snake eyes darting all about, sensing the surroundings like a forked tongue. "Quite an improvement. That's a nice kitty, so calm and clean. Now we'll see what we can do." He displayed a hideous grin.

"We? You insolent lummox! Do? I can't do a thing. Figure this one out yourself."

"Enough out of you. I've got to get your boy MacKenna to give back what he stole."

"Patrick, steal? He's as honest as the day is long."

"If I don't get those ledgers from the safe, your days won't be long at all."

"You mean those moldy old books? What difference will they make now, a hundred years later?"

"Plenty of difference — and trouble for Outfit. I've let Patrick know what I want. Now we wait."

Chapter Twenty-One

Kitty fell silent. Candicci led her into his small parlor and sat in a wooden armchair with a padded back and seat at a writing desk. Cigarette smoke hung low and made the cramped space feel even smaller. The room's spare furnishings consisted of two floor lamps, a threadbare couch, another armchair like his, and a low, glass-topped coffee table. She chose the chair. There was no phone in the room except the cell phone he held while he messaged someone, or played tic-tac-toe, for all she knew. She maintained her silence and waited for him to become even more uncomfortable than she. Why must everyone stay hypnotized in front of a screen, not talking to each other anymore?

Facing the couch on a low bookcase sat an older model flat screen television, which he kept on all the time. As he fiddled on his phone he glanced occasionally at the screen. FIX news showed a video clip of a huge rally in Houston's Cow Palace. She wasn't paying much attention — she'd heard it all. Some cocky fat guy was inciting a crowd of thousands of cheering fans. Many held up signs. A band beside the podium played a continuous background, accentuating the speaker's comments like the organ player at a baseball game,.

"How can you listen to that malarkey?" she asked.

Patrick had explained this to her. Hard as he'd worked for his independence — from his uncle, from Jason Holdroyd and from the politicians who would like to reshape his designs, it seemed he could never shake loose. Even as the Irish saw beyond politicians who told them how to vote, big decisions still came down to the Golden Rule — he who has the gold makes the rule.

His main driving force was his architectural vision. He remained true to his goals — to design buildings, as the old sage said, with Commodity, Firmness and Delight. This meant they must be functional, structurally sound, and beautiful. the classic requirements of architecture. But why did he work so hard on thankless tasks for low pay to make this happen?

He owed a lot to others who helped him — including Chet, Jason Holdroyd, the office staff, and the public. He returned the favor by devoting himself to hard work and took big risks — even solved crimes — for a reason. He wanted to do the right thing.

Even the ideals of the U. S. Constitution, the freedoms which had given his family better opportunities than they had in their native land, were disappearing. The world had changed, with an out-sized influence of the super-rich, corporate lobbyists, and so-called "facts" posted on the free internet, which spread like wildfire. Many in younger, and even older, generations enjoyed their freedom but would not lift a finger to protect their liberty, not even troubling to vote for those who had fought to preserve it. This entitled attitude had permitted widespread abuse of the political system.

The result was a political world driven by money, extreme points of view, and greedy, power-hungry politicians. The vision of America's opportunity had dimmed, and the ideas of hard work, compromise on conflicts, and joint effort that made the country great had begun to disappear.

"How can you listen to that nonsense?" she persisted.

"If more people paid attention," he said, "we'd be better off. He'll run the country like the Outfit."

"That's exactly what I'm afraid of," Kitty said. "You think he'll be your man, but he is only out for himself, like your boss Jimmy Romo."

"Shut your trap about Jimmy!"

"Just as Romo did," Kitty said, "the thugs of society are taking over."

"Don't spout off on things you know nothing about." He checked his Rolex. "I guess it's about lunchtime. We have mortadella sandwiches — Italian Bologna — or, peanut butter and jelly."

"I've had enough baloney lately, so I guess I'll go for the other. We don't often get peanuts where I come from — Ireland, don't you know?"

"I'll fix something up. Don't move."

"Well, I can't exactly go anywhere," she said. "Seems I misplaced my car keys, and you don't have any donkey carts available."

He scowled and left the room. Although he was opening up, this uptight sourpuss wasn't going to be much fun.

Her stomach growled in anticipation. Eventually he returned and set a plate of sandwiches, a dented apple and a cup of the lukewarm morning coffee on the table. Despite the plainness of the fare, she grabbed a sandwich, devoured it instantly and reached for another, washing it down with sour coffee. She finished off the apple as well.

"You've got quite an appetite for such a little thing," he said.

"I didn't eat much yesterday and — you know the rest." She wasn't ready to get into what was causing her outsized appetite. It would probably just make her more vulnerable to his manipulation.

"You have to accept us more," he continued. "All you have to do is what your bosses tell you. Nobody goes hungry, we take care of everyone's families, and we all stay happy."

"Yeah, I've noticed. Patrick has to bend over backwards to make sure he keeps your guys satisfied."

"We are all content because we all think alike. Differences cause conflicts. You know that, don't you, my dear?"

Oh, fiddle dee dee, here comes the party line. "First of all, I am not your dear. Secondly, I am quite different from you and choose to remain so."

"Since you are part of the family until Patrick comes to his senses and follows our orders, I 'm just reminding you of my orders."

"What are these orders? Patrick has fulfilled every expectation Joe had about the hotel and casino project. I don't believe he's obligated to you at all."

"All he has to do is return those ledgers and notes he stole. It's very simple."

"He would never steal your money, I can tell you that. But if it's something else that rightfully belongs to you, I'm sure a return can be arranged."

"Very well, Miss Kitty. I just wanted you to understand, I'm under orders too."

"Then, as a member of the 'family,' I am entitled to be properly fed, with what is generally considered good nutrition. While I appreciate your efforts, they fall far short of that simple requirement."

"Okay, okay, Just tell me what you want."

"Lobster with drawn butter would be nice," she teased.

"Other than that." The corners of his mouth turned upward in the trace of a smile, and his dark eyes warmed to a soft brown.

"Very well, let's make a list," he said.

"First of all, I need some milk, fat-free would be best. Then fruit — grapes, bananas, pears or oranges — whatever looks good in the store. And vegetables, like green beans, leaf lettuce, tomatoes, cucumbers, broccoli, and fresh wheat bread — real food, don't you know?"

"I hate broccoli."

"Then get cauliflower."

"Ugh." He wrote it down anyway. "Okay, I've got it."

"I certainly hope so. I'm used to eating better."

He finished his list, returned Kitty to her private quarters, and locked the door. With his smoke confined to the rest of the apartment, she opened the window to let in the temperate afternoon air and breathed easily for the first time since yesterday.

Chapter Twenty-Two

Kitty sat with Marco again in the smoky living room. Candicci still smarted from his dressing down by his bosses. But he hadn't told Kitty.

"It's so stuffy in here she said. How can you breathe?" she said.

"Oh, you get used to it."

"You sure smoke a lot — is that a chronic cough?"

"Only at night, when I lie down."

"That's the most important time to breathe easily, so you can fall asleep."

"Ha! That's when I tense up — all the problems of the day running through my mind."

"I've never seen you relax," Kitty remarked.

"That's why I smoke. It helps me to calm down."

"Aren't you afraid of lung cancer?"

"In my line of work that's the least of my worries."

"Maybe that's why I never see you smile."

He was silent for a full minute. Finally, he turned to her and snarled. "You know, the trouble with you bitches is — where do I start?" It turned out he had been ruminating all this time, grasping to express a thought with an extremely limited vocabulary.

"What is your problem with women? You're so harsh and nasty where I am concerned."

"A woman is a big expense and nothing but trouble."

"So you do without them?"

"That's none of your business!" he snapped. "Besides in my line of work, they take too much time — and I'm never there."

"Now we're getting somewhere. What about all the great loves in history — like Lancelot and Guinevere? Somehow, they survived long separations."

"Maybe I'm not dreamboat material — romance isn't my long suit."

He was helpless to express feelings, but at least his gambling vocabulary helped him find the words.

"Did you ever think about getting married?" She pressed further.

He remained silent and looked absently out the window. At last, he spoke.

"Ah, Morena!" He sighed. "She was my last conquest, if you could call it that — a dark-haired Hispanic beauty with a body that wouldn't quit."

"That's a quaint expression — I never heard it in Ireland."

"Sorry" He blushed. "She had an active mind and an endless, uh, love of life. She liked to spend money on clothes, wine and fancy restaurants. We were crazy about each other."

"What happened?"

"We were getting serious. She wanted me to take a different job and settle down. I balked."

"Why? Sounds like it's what you both wanted."

"I can't just walk away from the mob — it's for life. Besides, I could never find another way to earn so much money. She wanted me to buy a house, stay in one place and come home for dinner every night."

"It sounds normal — that's what I want."

"And… and she wanted to have children. I couldn't face that."

"You are daft! Who in heaven's name wouldn't want that? That's my dream. Patrick and I are just starting our family and— " She hesitated. "I'm expecting a baby."

"Ooph!" He doubled over as if he had been punched. Soon his shoulders began to shake.

What was his hangup with children? She had exposed a lot of raw emotion in this repressed personality. She wanted to know more but was afraid to pry further, fearing he would release it all at one time, with unpredictable results.

"My God!' He stood and turned toward the kitchen. "It's lunchtime, and I haven't even prepared anything."

Way too late, he realized he had played it all wrong. He had charged down one path—the wrong one — and now he could never win her respect.

"Now that you mention it, I'm hungry again — I am always hungry these days. Eating for two has become a full-time thing."

A few minutes later he reappeared with a plate of sandwiches, a glass of milk and the rest of a bag of potato chips. She was tired of peanut butter and decided to try the mortadella.

"This sandwich is good. What's that dressing you put on it?"

"It's called muffaletta spread, basically a tapenade, with chopped olives, olive oil and Italian seasonings."

"Delicious. Where did you learn to make Italian specialties?"

"My mama. She was a good cook, taught me lots of recipes. She used to say, "A man who can cook will never go hungry."

"Used to?"

"She died when I was twelve. My dad used to beat her, until one day — ,"

"He went too far?"

"He was convicted for her beating death and went to prison. I went to foster care. When I was old enough to leave. I hit the streets. Then he died. The outfit is my only family now."

"So sorry, Marco. What a bum break."

She was befriending him now, treating him like a real human being. It felt good. But the game was up. It would all end soon. Somehow she knew.

Candicci stood abruptly and disappeared into the kitchen.

Chapter Twenty-Three

Patrick called Chet into his office. When he closed the door like this, he needed to talk.

"I know Candicci can't return to the mob house up the street. But I have no idea where he has taken Kitty. Our only clues are the phone numbers I found in the mob hideout. I called them found they were disconnected. The area code was that new one they're assigning to outlying suburbs. "

"The last time he tried taking hostages," Chet said, "it turned into a fiasco that worked in your favor."

"We can't risk a raid like that one — not with Kitty in her present condition."

"Where do we start looking?"

"He needs something — he'll call."

Chet loved crime fiction and movies, where crime didn't pay. This was real life — no such luck guaranteed. Patrick managed to scare the hell out of him.

Soon enough Patrick's instincts proved correct. On the third day after Kitty's abduction, Patrick received a text message on his cell phone: "We have your wife. Get terms of release at Joe's Little Place, 9:00 PM tonight. DO NOT CALL POLICE."

Patrick knew the place only too well — this was where Joe Bohannon kept his office and often hung out during the day. Despite the danger, he would have to risk going there without telling O'Malley. It was a hangout for some of Joe's least savory cronies. Normally Patrick avoided it at all costs. As insurance in case he disappeared, he called Nick McGurk with a heads up. He informed him where he'd be in the evening.

Nick got Gloria on the line. "Patrick, this is ridiculous," she said. What does he think you are, a mob messenger service?"

"I don't care what he thinks, "Patrick said "He's got to let Kitty go.?"

"We're all supposed to be working together."

"Jimmy Romo is in town," Nick said, "and he has put the heat on Candicci over some stupid missing account books. Kitty is in no condition to be a pawn in this senseless game."

"Look, Gloria," Patrick said. "This is my only way to free Kitty. He also wants fifrty-grand. What would you suggest?"

"You go ahead and attend the meeting. Forge the money. I'm going to call Pop and end this nonsense right now. But don't talk with anyone until you stop in the back and check in with Pop first."

At nine p.m. on the dot Patrick, toting his battered briefcase, pushed open the door of Joe's Little Place in Bucktown on the North Side. From previous visits he had a nodding acquaintance with the bartender, who inclined his head toward the back corner, where a tall man in an expensive suit sat in a booth. It was Candicci himself, nursing a beer. Patrick turned his head away, walked past his table and knocked softly on Joe's office door. He half expected no response, since he had only met with Joe here in the daytime.

"Come in," came Bohannon's voice through the door panel.

Entering, Patrick was surprised to find Jimmy Romo sitting in Joe's best guest chair.

"Hi Joe — and Mr. Romo, I haven't seen you in a few years. Am I interrupting something?"

"No. Now we can begin," Romo spoke with a harsh snarl. "Get Candicci in here."

Patrick backed out the office door and beckoned for Candicci to come in and join them.

He entered the office. Patrick followed.

"Joe, Jimmy, what the hell is going on?" Candicci stared from one boss to the other in startled dismay.

"That's what we want to know, Marco," Bohannon said.

"What the hell do you think you're doing?" Romo said.

"Just following orders. You want the ledgers, and I'm determined to get them back for you, plus fifty grand for her safe return."

"Why you stupid son of a bitch! What's with the cash," Romo asked, "a generous tip for your genius strategy?"

"No, it was for you!"

"Sure, sure. I have half a notion to give you up on this kidnapping rap, but it's too messy. Either you drive Kitty in good condition to Gloria's office by 9 AM tomorrow morning, or your ass is grass and I'm the lawnmower. Then you keep on driving until you get to my office in Detroit, and you stay there where I can keep an eye on you until I say otherwise."

"In case you don't this man's his drift," Joe said, "we're going to put you on ice for a while, until this blows over."

Candicci, his shirt bathed in sweat, was reduced to a sniveling reply. "Yes, sir. May I go now?"

"Get back to Kitty and make sure she's well provided for until morning," Romo continued. "And no funny business!"

Candicci slithered out through the tap room, his head bowed, his eyes glued to the ground, ignoring the stares of curious bar customers.

When the meeting resumed, Romo wanted to know what happened to the ledgers and notebook. "Did you see them, MacKenna?"

"I did. I found them in the old safe in the house. They were ancient mob history, all the way back to Capone and Curly Humphries, plus the more recent notebook. I removed them from the safe. I gave them all to Gloria for their historical interest."

"Where are they now?" Romo asked.

"When she was interviewed about the murder of Charles Simmons, she surrendered them all to the FBI."

Jimmy groaned.

"It'll be all right, Jimmy," Joe sat back in his chair and shook his head. "My own daughter… but she did the right thing."

"I didn't foresee that!" Patrick said. "If this helps, I had a copy made of everything, and I'm happy to present it to you." He set his briefcase on a chair and took out three stacks of paper, still in the envelopes from the print shop, and set them on the front of Joe's desk.

"Too late, too late," Romo said, accepting the stack of envelopes. "Oh. My. God!"

Chapter Twenty-Four

Gloria and Patrick sat at the kitchen table at the Rockville farmhouse finishing their second cup of coffee. As Jimmy Romo demanded, Candicci showed up with his hostage at nine a.m.

Patrick met her tat the front door and embraced her. "Kitty, to think I almost lost you!"

Gloria joined them in the hall. Kitty said, "I don't know what you did, but thank you!"

"You didn't deserve that. The fear thing had gone far enough — all over some stupid old records!"

Marco Candicci squirmed in his unique way, observing the tender scene in disbelief, a silent witness to the devotion he had so savagely disrupted. "I better get the hell out of here. If they catch up with me, I'm toast — and Jimmy would likely let me rot in jail." He left as quickly as he'd come.

Gloria ushered them into the parlor, where they sat.

Little Mike ran up to her and climbed on her mother's lap. Gloria smoothed his hair.

"Unca Pat," he gurgled, waving to him.

"He's so cute — I can't take my eyes off him." Kitty's grin was so wide her face hurt. "I can hardly believe I'll have my own beautiful child pretty soon."

Patrick lifted the toddler off Gloria's lab. "It's good we're all back together again. Do you have a kiss for Auntie Kitty?" Little Mike reached for her face as Patrick lowered him toward her. He gave her a wet smack.

"The four of us — we seem like one happy family," Kitty said. "I hope we can always get together like this."

"Right," Patrick said. "I hope so."

"Gloria, I can't express enough gratitude for my rescue."

Kind as Gloria wanted to be, old feelings were standing in the way. She'd never fully accepted Kitty, denying her the bond she craved.

Patrick stood little Mike on his own feet and turned to Kitty. "We'd better get moving. Radi and O'Malley are headed this way to interview Gloria.. I especially want to keep you away from those brutes for now. You need some quiet time at home."

"You'd be surprised," Kitty said. "I can handle some pretty rough types."

As they were leaving, Patrick turned to his ex-fiancé. "Gloria, I'm sure you'll manage, with your usual grace and firmness."

"Right, just leave it to the women." She winked at Kitty.

Chapter Twenty-Five

Kitty's curiosity got Patrick thinking. The next morning as he and Chet met in his office to discuss the workload, he was still pondering their discussion.

"How society did get so reckless, undisciplined, and careless of their precious political heritage," Patrick said. "You and I weren't brought up that way, and neither was Kitty."

"My dad grew up in the fifties and sixties," Chet said. "His pictures from back then show him with long hair, tie-dyed shirts and bell-bottom pants. He showed me his 'Make Love Not War' buttons and his silver chain with an Ahnk symbol ♀ — a nice one in hand-modeled silver."

"As I understand it," Patrick said, "President Eisenhower had served after World War II to calm and refocus society on civilian prosperity and growth."

"But by the end of his second term," Chet said, "young people were restless and considered government capable of doing more to improve society and the world. Dad said they even had a joke: 'What does an Eisenhower doll do?' Answer: 'You wind it up and it sits there and does nothing for eight years.'

"And then John F. Kennedy, Jr., who was much closer to their age than the retired general, came along and was nominated as the Democratic candidate for president. With his youth and optimism, he led the country to a changed and visionary destiny. He was considered winner of a series of three televised political debates, the first in our history, with his rival candidate Richard Nixon. He pointed out they could do something important. But he hadn't hit upon a formula that would capture the imagination of young people and turn them out to vote.

"Dad said that, at the beginning of the 1960 political campaign, Chester Bowles, former ambassador to India and U.S. Congressman from Connecticut, appeared at that campus on behalf of Kennedy. A student asked him how they could put the candidate's challenge into action. Bowles mentioned that his own son and daughter-in-law were currently helping to build a school in Nigeria. The idea caught fire with students, and they backed Kennedy as the one who could show them how to make a difference.

"Then in October 1960, when Kennedy addressed students at the University of Michigan, he challenged them with his now famous words, 'Ask not what your country can do for you; ask what you can do for your country.' As soon as Kennedy won, he formed the Peace Corps, a channel for serving one's country in a constructive, nonmilitary role."

"The Peace Corps was a great idea," Patrick said. "It was a diplomatic way to help numerous countries around the world. It spread a good impression of Americans in those countries, without politically controversial military intervention."

"Today, those public-spirited times have disappeared,' Patrick said, "It seems to me, if we look at the psychology that holds the mob together, we'll know a lot or about today's strange public attitudes and modern politics. These populist politicians turn everything around and blame their political opponents for their own shortcomings, like the sex addict who preaches against prostitution. For every crime or unpopular policy they are guilty of — like sexual transgressions, dirty politics, or bad government decisions — they falsely blame their critics. As part of their inner circle, what the mob would call his 'family,' they promise to protect them from all that. Those people who have already surrendered their loyalty to him fall in love with their captor and don't question their lies.

This makes politicians feel better about their excesses and crimes, but it doesn't stop them from committing them."

"Maybe so," Chet said, "but that brings me back to the present. Now that Kitty is back, how do we solve our immediate problems?"

"Which ones?" Patrick said. "I've got a lot on my mind." He thought about how he could level with Kitty. She didn't know the facts, although she could have guessed. The truth about him and Gloria sat like a lump of lead in his gut, weighing him down every day. If he could break it to her gently, she might understand more about Gloria's feelings toward her. If he could not, his whole world might come crashing down in an instant.

For the moment, he would also set aside his deepening conflict with Chet over the suitability of the Victorian house and its neighborhood as an affordable, pleasant place to live and raise a family. Chet's objections to proceeding with the purchase were mounting in proportion to the rising cost of making the Victorian mansion livable. Still, there were plenty of other unresolved matters Patrick was willing to discuss with his colleague and best friend.

"The most pressing issue is how to keep the project moving." Chet said. "Joe is dealing with mob issues — keeping Candicci at bay and preventing Detroit from invading his Chicago turf. Meanwhile, our subcontractors are screaming to get paid. If the gaming machine contractors walk off the job, we won't be able to open.

"You should talk to your uncle about this," Chet continued. "He's the one who got us into this project, and he knows how to handle both Joe and the subcontractors. He ought to be able to shake loose more cash and keep everyone happy."

"You're right Chet!" Patrick acted surprised and pleased, as if this were a new idea that had never occurred to him. "I owe him my monthly construction report anyway."

Chapter Twenty-Six

When he returned to the office Patrick called his uncle, who for the past six months had been setting up an office in St. Louis and seeking new business.

"Mike, how are you doing down there?"

"I'm so busy I don't know which way to turn."

"That's usually good news."

"I'm driving these architects crazy with new jobs. They're up to capacity and can't take anything else."

"You could send us some work up here. We have a big staff and could handle more."

"Down here, it's all about relationships. If you can't hold their hands and handle their requests personally, they resent it and go to somebody who will. You'll have to see it to understand. How about you? Are you busy?"

"The hotel is almost finished. Your team is painting the last hotel rooms, and the casino is being completed as quickly as we can get the electronics installed and working."

"Rudy reports regularly to me, but you're the architect — I need your observations. How does it look?"

"Your painters are good. Also, as Rudy can tell you, grading is proceeding on our teahouse island and stage and for the amphitheater on the other side of the channel."

"Are they getting it right? You haven't told me much."

"Yes, but there's a problem with cash flow. The subcontractors' monthly payments are two weeks overdue. They're all unhappy. And if those gaming machine techs walk out, we'll be delayed months on the opening."

"Oh crap, I'm so busy with new work I forgot to sign and return the Application and Certificate for Payment. It's buried . . . right here on my desk. I'll Fedex it out right away."

"Thanks, Joe—much appreciated.

"I'll call Nick and tell him to expedite the checks today. Better yet, I'll put him in charge of approving these requests. He's there, anyway — it'll speed things up."

"Great idea. You and Rose okay?"

"We're loving this town. Has Kitty been released from that lowlife yet?"

"Yes, this week. What a relief! I haven't even had a chance to call. I've been distracted by her kidnapping—I have a lot to tell you." He filled him in on Kitty's kidnapping and release.

"Aww, man, you two need a break Why don't you and Kitty come down here? You can stay at our beautiful new home. I'll also introduce you to the architects I work with down here. They're planning to expand. I know they're anxious to meet you."

"I could see us getting away for a few days next week. I can call some of it business development and the rest just a bit of vacation. We could sure use it."

At home that night Patrick asked Kitty, "How would you like a few days' vacation in St. Louis — to visit Mike and Rose and see the sights?"

"Kitty's eyes lit up. "Really, can we go?"

"We can leave on the weekend."

"But what about my work? It's St. Patrick's Day weekend, our busiest time of the year."

"I've already asked Ma an Pa to cover for you — they said those kids you've trained will take care of things just fine, just as they did when you were gone."

"Then, of course! How exciting!"

"Then it's set. Let's leave early Saturday morning."

At dinner Patrick brought up Chet's cultural summary of the 1960s with Kitty. and explained to her his theory of how it was affecting the present day.

"I'm trying to understand what Gloria is doing to escape from the mob. The most important thing I've noticed," he said, "is that she and Nick are gaining financial independence from the gang with their business success."

"They wouldn't be making nearly as much progress," Kitty noted, "without Nick's natural talent for business and her ability to charm her customers."

"True. In addition, they both have relationships with Detroit's Jimmy Romo that extend back many years. Nick loves and protects Gloria. I'm hoping he knows Jimmy well enough to overcome his attempts to take over Chicago Joe's operations. It's so easy to see how closely the current right wing politicians act like mobsters."

"You keep saying that. Why?" she said.

"To begin with, they both take in followers who are outcasts: disappointed or disgruntled people, who feel excluded from the mainstream of society. They act as a family for them, non-judgmental and accepting. As long as they do the boss's bidding without question, the can even advance in the organization. Think about who they include.: old white guys, who feel threatened by the advancement of women, Blacks, Hispanics and Asians in our society. Self-righteous women, who feel their view of women's role is the only correct one and that everyone ought to conform to their beliefs, opinions and behavior. Also, loners identify with these leaders' anti-society attitudes and take them a step further and commit criminal acts in hopes of pleasing them. And the super-wealthy contribute millions to win over these voters. Then they shape government policy to favor their own interests."

"A bunch of silly man with no common sense," Kitty said. They ought to put a woman in charge!"

Chapter Twenty-Seven

On the weekend Patrick and Kitty set off by car on their a sightseeing and business break in St. Louis. They stayed with Uncle Mike and Auntie Rose. Unknown to Patrick, Kitty had called Rose and arranged a St. Patrick's Day surprise party in his honor.

Rose served corned beef, cabbage,, potatoes and all the trimmings. Kitty even found a new recipe for shamrock pie, with a chocolate chip and pudding filling, a flaky crust, and whipped cream topping, drizzled with bright green crème de menthe.

They moved to the spacious living room for the final touch. Mike served Irish coffee, each cup with sugar cubes, a shot of Paddy Irish whiskey and more whipped cream topping. Kitty had made a tall Dr. Seuss hat for Patrick, with white and green horizontal stripes, which he proudly wore as the guest of honor on his name day, and a necklace of green beads with a dangling shamrock pendant.

"It's so good to have you here," Rose said. "When we get together in Chicago, there's usually so much going on — either work at the pub or so many people to see — that we have not had much chance to talk, especially with you, Kitty."

"I know, Rose. I feel the same way. How did you and Mike meet?"

"They had a dance at our parish church, St. Finn Barr's, and they invited all of the junior and senior girls at the convent school I attended. Since you're from Cork, I suppose you've heard of it, run by Sacred Heart nuns."

"Heard of it? I attended it myself, a few years later, of course. I loved it, especially my favorite teacher, Mother O'Brien."

"Oh, for heaven's sake! Meghan O'Brien was there, all right, as a member of my class. The two of us were thick as thieves — we plagued the nuns with all manner of devilish tricks.

"It was a wonderful era to be there," Rose continued. "The Society of the Sacred Heart nuns in the convent were modern. During that time the Pope proclaimed his Vatican II encyclical. They adopted conventional dress for their shopping, speaking, and charity calls and mingled freely with the people of the town. We students addressed them by their actual surnames. Mother O'Brien, as she is called, became an English teacher. This women's order was most closely comparable to the men's order of intellectual Jesuits. They were in touch with world affairs and held modern views of society. They taught history, social studies, and a wide sampling of the literary canon — stories, especially those with spiritual elements, in true Irish tradition."

"What a grand coincidence! I feel as if I already know you," Kitty said. "You may recall how much she loved mysteries, and we read Edgar Allen Poe in class. In fact, one of his stories led us to important clues in solving the mysteries of the house we have been trying to buy."

Mike made a second round of Irish coffee for everyone and proposed a toast. "Here's to St. Patrick, and his namesake, of course. He drove the snakes from Ireland and served as an inspiration for all the Patricks to come!" They raised their cups and sipped.

"And let's drink to ridding Chicago of one particular snake, who's doing penance in Detroit, we hope, for his unruly and unlawful conduct. May he never return." They drank.

This led to the topic of their adventures in buying the historic Victorian mansion. Patrick resumed the narrative and told of his hopes, dreams, and excitement for the new project.

"Sounds like a heap of difficulties, just to have a nice place to live," Mike said.

"My goodness, you could build your own home more easily, right here in Woodlawn," Rose said. She couldn't contain their enthusiasm for the place as a new home for the couple. "There are some beautiful lots just up the street. Think how many obstacles you could avoid,"

Mike, as a contractor, usually favored the "tear it down and start over" approach. "No murders, no expensive historic restoration, and a home layout to suit yourselves!"

"Oh Patrick," Kitty said. "That is so tempting. You could design the house exactly the way we both want. I love the old house in Chicago, but there are so many hoops to jump through before we can move in."

"There are good schools and a lovely creek running past all the lots," Rose said.

"It's certainly something to think about," Patrick said. "Meanwhile, we have obligations back in Chicago, and I'm reluctant to leave my parents, who need our help at the pub."

"You should've thought of that when you decided to become an architect," Kitty said.

"In fact," Patrick admitted, "I did discuss this with my parents at the time I decided on an architectural career. They gave their consent and encouraged me all along the way. They are resigned to continuing without me and have made plans to do so,""

"At least let me introduce you to my friends at Childress & Marx, architects and engineers. You would fit right in with them, and they desperately need to expand. They're looking for someone bold, creative, and resourceful like you. They would be so lucky if you decided to join them!"

"I've been wanting to meet them, and it's long overdue. Go ahead and set it up. Maybe we can help each other somehow. Still, aside from you, most of my business contacts remain in Chicago."

Chapter Twenty-Eight

The next day Mike took Patrick to the downtown offices of the architecture and engineering firm, Childress & Marx, to meet Lewis Childress, President and founding architect in the partnership. He drove to the parking lot in back of the old Union Station. Today it still hosted trains along a few of the original tracks.

From their parking space they entered the lobby of a a ten-story office tower, pushed the button for an upper floor, where the receptionist conducted them to the corner office.

Mike rapped on the frame of the open door. Childress stood and walked forward to meet his guests. "Here we are, Lew. May I present Patrick MacKenna and his wife Kitty?"

"At long last!" Childress boomed. "It's such a pleasure to meet you both."

"It's been far too long, I know, Mr. Childress. But Mike here keeps us so busy with his projects, I can barely find time to get home for dinner with Kitty in the evening."

"Oh, call me Lew, for heaven's sake." He looked the part of senior partner, with a full head of snowy hair, Of medium height, with a matching mustache and beard, he made a cheery, Santa Claus impression, yet his athletic build was stocky and fit, suggesting he worked out on a regular basis.

He led them on a tour around an aisle that formed a rectangular doughnut around the space, introducing a couple of department heads who were not busy with staff. He noted the locations of each department: architecture; planning, and civil, structural, mechanical, and electrical engineering. A large area was devoted to staffers in marketing and business development. At the center of the building's north wall a glass partition enclosed a large conference room. He proudly conducted them through a clear glass entry door, where a dozen chrome and leather chairs surrounded a long conference table and invited them to sit. From this vantage they could enjoy a spectacular panorama of the entire downtown, from Arch to expressway, spanned from the Gateway Arch on the river to Union Station. It took in the new St. Louis Blues arena and several other construction sites the recent activity had stimulated in the newer, western portion of downtown.

Childress took a moment to describe downtown progress. A U.S. 40/I-64 off-ramp framed the view on the left. The new ice hockey arena and its parking structure appeared next. On the near Side of Market Street, was Maggie O'Brien's, a beloved Irish pub and restaurant. Across a side street, the historic Union Station occupied an entire city block adjoining vaulted train shed.

Redeveloped, the wide-span roof sheltered restaurants, shops, and an aquarium. Still, at one side remained an Amtrak train station bound for distant cities. But most of the large space, Childress explained, had been converted to an entertainment venue, with shops and cafés and a new hotel within and around offering space for private meetings, weddings and parties, This new visitor attraction also featured a fudge stand, he explained. As these confectioners made their product, their synchronized rap routine, with scheduled show times, attracted large crowds to watch. Further east lay the original downtown, with its French Renaissance City Hall, a 1930s limestone-faced federal courts building and the main post office.

Over coffee and pastries, the senior firm principal described his hopes for the future of the firm. In some ways their organization resembled Holdroyd & Robb. Both companies had illustrious histories and were actively engaged in government, commercial and industrial projects. The St. Louis firm, however, seemed a little further advanced in developing new business for the expanding metropolis, which now covered eight urban counties in Missouri and Illinois and had a population of three million people. Childress had gotten to know a few members of the group formerly known as Civic Progress — an elite committee of local corporate CEOs, who had steered the region's development from behind the scenes over many years. It was an influential body of movers and shakers who had backed key projects, such as the Gateway Arch, major downtown improvements, and future development initiatives.

"It pays to know their goals and objectives and to keep them informed about the merits of our own development programs," he said. "By working with them, we've been able to move our top priority projects ahead.

"That's where you come in, Patrick. If you decided to move here, we would make a spot for you as good or better than at your present firm, as head of our architectural group, which has even greater potential for growth."

"It sounds as if you've hitched your wagon to very important forces in getting new business," Patrick said to his host. "This gives me a lot to think about."

They parted graciously and spent the rest of the weekend visiting the top of the Arch, the zoo and the art museum. Patrick was even a little reluctant to begin the drive home, leave this lovely place, and return to noisy, bustling Chicago, fraught with all the problems they would face immediately on their return

134

Chapter Twenty-Nine

Back home again, Kitty faced the challenge of re-planning the house. At dinner Patrick brought it up first.

"Now that Candicci and Romo are out of the way for the time being, maybe we'll have a chance to study the house in peace."

"I want to revisit the house with its former occupant, Henley Wilson. Kitty said, "to learn more about his and Charlie's plans to renovate the house.

"Good idea," Patrick said. "I can ask him about the mob's intrusion into the house and get his take on what these crooks are looking for."

"I'd even like to bring Gloria along, to see what good ideas she has about restoring and adapting the rooms to our current needs."

"Well, if you insist." Patrick said. "But I'm pretty sure she might feel differently about how to re-use the house than we do."

"Still, she has a good eye for design. Besides, I'd like to know her better and would like her to feel closer to us."

"Saturday would probably be the best day for it."

Thus encouraged, using the floor plans, during evenings at home Kitty sketched out room layouts, while Patrick made separate lists describing proposed work for each trade: electricians, plumbers, and heating-cooling contractors. He planned to use the hidden rooms for concealing mechanical equipment and to open up the tower as a back stair and second fire exit from the house.

At work the next morning Patrick described the forthcoming tour to Chet. "What do you think?"

Chet shook his head. "Lots of luck with that one!" He pointed out that this was making a complex project even more difficult. He still had major concerns about tackling the project in the first place. Now Patrick insisted upon getting two different women's opinions at the same time — and he had a personal history with each of them. "What's the point of having Gloria there? They are bound to disagree. Then what do you do?"

"Kitty knows Gloria has a sense for good design," Patrick explained. "She did a wonderful job with the farmhouse. Maybe she'll have an inspiration that will bring the whole thing together."

"If that happens, what's going to bring you and Kitty together? If you like Gloria's concept, it won't be Kitty's idea and she'll hate living there. If you don't, your client Gloria is going to be angry with you. You're risking having two unhappy women on your hands."

Nonetheless, Patrick, stumped like many architects by an interior design challenge, felt each had something to contribute.

On Saturday Wilson, Kitty, Patrick and Gloria, who had left the toddler back at the farmhouse with Nick, met at the Bond Street property at ten o'clock.

When they assembled in the front hall on Saturday morning, Patrick introduced them to the surviving owner Hensley Wilson and suggested that he conduct a tour around the house. He began by describing what he and Charlie had in mind for its restoration and reuse. Since Patrick's last meeting with him, Wilson had recovered his composure. He wore Levi's, an emerald green T-shirt, and a black blazer. His parted blond hair swept across a broad forehead and almost covered one eye. He described their vision for restoration of the ground floor.

"We were in the process of removing the decorative carved blocks while retaining the oak rectangles forming the stair balustrade, a more modern touch which will simplify maintenance and cleaning while preserving its original form. We retained and cleaned the original brass and crystal chandelier as a centerpiece for the entry hall." He motioned for the group to enter the living room to the left of the stairwell.

"This parlor was to be our grand salon, for receiving guests and holding parties. After some experimentation, we found these island groupings to be the best for the furniture. We've been reupholstering and refinishing the original period pieces when we had time. As you can see, we never made it to restoration of the ceiling or the lighting fixtures, which we decided to keep."

Stepping through the wide archway to the room behind the parlor, Wilson said, "We got the dining room cleaned, replaced the wall covering, restored the original natural finishes on the woodwork, and repaired some of the furniture, which we fortunately acquired in the purchase. We found that the chandelier just needed a can of Brasso, some rags and a lot of elbow grease. The dining room was finally in usable condition." He indicated, through double twelve-light glass doors behind the dining room, an enclosed sun room containing two desks, bookcases and low filing cabinets, set up as their office.

He led the group toward the kitchen to the right of the dining room on the other side of the house. "The kitchen had been remodeled in the 1950s with some features which are still in demand today. It's an early postwar modernization, which has historic value in itself."

"All we'd have to do was replace the refrigerator and dishwasher," Patrick said, "and we could use it immediately."

"That's what we decided to do," Kitty said. "It is still worth preserving."

"I suppose it will have to do," Gloria said. "It would be costly to bring it up to date."

"That was the whole idea," Wilson said. "To save that expense, we were happy to leave it at another historical date. Now let's go upstairs."

They trooped up the main stairway and stood along the upstairs railing overlooking the stair hall. "We admired the stained-glass panel above the center run of stairs. There are a few cracked panes, but they're too beautiful to replace, so we intended to put clear storm panels outside to seal out the weather when we got the money,"

In the master bedroom suite, Wilson explained, they had wanted to change the decor from the depressing heavy furniture, dark woodwork and brocaded fabric on the walls to something more modern and cheerful. "We had hoped to suit the rooms to a layout closer to today's living patterns. For example, this alcove should have a comfortable seating group. These grim paintings should be replaced with brighter, lighter art: prints of Impressionists, for example."

"We hope to do that someday, but it's not a top priority," Patrick said. "It has some grandeur as it is now."

"Certainly, change the paintings," Gloria said. "but I would leave the room alone and restore it as is. Better lighting and fresh wall covering could do wonders for these rooms."

"I thought the alcove would be a lovely place for the baby's crib, and we could redecorate the adjacent room as a nursery. In any case,"I agree, these dour paintings will have to go. "

"You want to live in this house, you should live in a grand manner!" Gloria swept her arm wide.

"When you put it that, way, I suppose the house is telling us what we should do, isn't it?" Kitty said.

"It wants you to live up to it."

"Yes, I see what you mean." But clearly Kitty disagreed with Gloria's advice.

Patrick thanked all present, especially Hensley Wilson, and they all left but he and Kitty.

The tour was over, but not its message. Kitty didn't understand why Patrick hadn't left Gloria out of his personal decisions and moved on. She dwelt for some time on the obvious conflicts between her own hopes for the house and Gloria's sweeping decrees,

The house had a will of its own. It made demands, it had imperatives. "Restore me to what I was! Repair this, fix that."

She was beginning to realize what several friends had already pointed out. Many of these things had nothing to do with livability of the house, yet they were costing a bloody fortune. Questions bombarded her like a hailstorm. She wondered if Chet's opinion was right. Was their will to overcome adversity overtaking their common sense? When did the need to find a place to live begin to diverge so widely from the demands of restoring this house? Like frogs in slowly boiling water, had they lost their grip on reality? Was she losing her mind?

Chapter Thirty

Twilight descended on Bond Street. As Kitty beheld the wintry landscape, crows settled in the barren backyard oak for their vocal evening "caw-cus," as Patrick called it. Streetlights came on in futile combat against the gloom. A bat streaked across the darkening autumn sky in quest of the few insect morsels that survived.

Her mood was as dark as the grim scene before her. Inside, the table lamp and wall brackets cast a feeble light, which failed to brighten the dim, cavernous bedroom. While she had bared her soul to the love of her life, and she thought he had done the same, she trembled with an unknown fear. What secrets still remained? At last the right words bubbled to the surface.

"What in heaven's name is Gloria talking about?" Kitty demanded. "She thinks we should live in some 'grand manner.' Shouldn't I have a say in how we occupy this house? Since you left her for me, I've tried to be kind and gentle with Gloria, but now this. Why are you so dependent on her approval of our decisions?

"Why not? She knows more about interior design than I do."

"Maybe so, but not more that I do! Why does she have such influence over you?"

"She cares, Kitty. She wants to get to know.us, to have a nice place for her family to visit — to set a good example for Little Mike."

"Ah, so that's it! Nick seems like an ideal father to me. Tell me, what's your connection?"

Patrick blanched. His heart pounded. A warning screamed in his head. Did she know?

"Well, it's just that. . . "

"What about Gloria's casual marks about heredity — your hazel eyes, not blue? What am I supposed to do with that?"

His head was about to burst. He blurted, "Let me talk, for heaven's sake!"

"Out with it!. What were you going to tell me?"

"I can explain, "Patrick reached for her.

She shrunk away. "Well?"

"This was a situation which developed slowly. I only learned about it after you and I had found each other to be soulmates, after we were engaged."

Kitty fell silent, listening.

"After I had solved the mystery of the office building murder and had met you, I left Gloria. But I was concerned that her father Joe Bohannon might be unhappy with me over our breakup. I was afraid he would fire me, and I couldn't finish designing the hotel project. You already know I considered this job my first big break — the chance of a lifetime for a young architect."

"What what's that got to do with it?" Kitty breathed faster and her heart pounded. "You're giving me excuses without telling me what you are trying to excuse."

"Please, I'm not finished." Patrick said. "Then Joe announced that his wife Candy and his daughter Gloria had decided to take a long-postponed trip to Europe, which they had always longed to do. Joe could never risk being away for such a long time. He was delighted and relieved that his wife and daughter would be happily occupied, while he and I would be free to focus on the complicated job of designing and building the casino and hotel. I was relieved that Gloria had no lasting hard feelings about breaking up with me and was taking a long, interesting trip while she thought about her future."

"Yes, yes, I knew all about that at the time."

"It was only when she came back that I understood. She had a baby boy with her, and it was hers and mine."

Chapter Thirty-One

It took Patrick some time to calm Kitty down enough to get her in the car and drive her home. Back at their Lake Shore Drive apartment Kitty was inconsolable — crying, then silent, then bursting out in gut-wracking sobs.

She wanted to grill Patrick on the details of when and how he learned of his fatherhood. She tried to remain calm and coldly unemotional. Only with difficulty could she begin asking more.

"I have always been open with you. I've never held back stories about my troubles. I don't understand why you couldn't do the same."

"I could hardly tell you what I didn't even know. I felt fortunate that Gloria was not angry over our breakup. By going on her trip she was giving me a chance to devote a lot of time to our new project."

"I can't blame you for that. But how could you let it happen in the first place? Just when our new life is starting so well, you're dragging me back into your old one."

"Nick McGurk came along at the perfect time for Gloria. He adores her, respects her and is thrilled to become part of her life! He'll be a wonderful husband and father."

"Lucky for you!" You land on your feet, and I'm left in the dark."

"I could never love her the way Nick does. She loves to be with people, always talking, laughing and trading stories. Her idea of an interesting evening is having all of her club women over to gossip, compare their clothes and amuse each other. You know me, I think we both like to read, think, study and watch good movies. I need a few good friends — she needs dozens. You're my companion in all those things. We belong together."

"Isn't that just so great for Gloria? As usual, she leads a charmed life, while the rest of us pay the price. What about me? And you — I can't deal with it." She began crying again.

"Now, Kitty, be reasonable. What could I do?"

"Do? What about honesty? I can't live with you any longer. Patrick, you deceived me. I don't trust you anymore." She stood abruptly and stared into the watery gloom.

The dimly lit apartment was surrounded by blackness. She felt she was floating in space. It took a moment for her eyes to adjust. The view was grim indeed — dark grey clouds scudded in a brisk north wind. Horizontal rain drummed on the floor-to-ceiling windows. Her emotions peaked, mirroring the turmoil over the lake

"I'm leaving!"

"You can't go now. Look at this gale! You'll have to wait until morning."

Furious, Kitty retired to the master bedroom, slammed the door and locked it. In futility Patrick retired to his study to spend the night alone.

Kitty tossed for an hour in her bed, her thoughts racing. She couldn't sleep and called Sarah, one of the first friends she made in her immigrant group and her former roommate at the girls' dormitory. She packed a small bag with essentials. She put on her winter parka, held Buster and her small tote bag in her arms, and tiptoed silently past the door of Patrick's study. When the elevator reached the lobby, fighting a stiff wind against the glass door, she leaned outward on it until it blew open. She set Buster down and held his leash as he shivered in the tiny square of sodden grass at ground level. She called for a Lyft ride and waited for it at the curb in the cold, windy downpour.

Chapter Thirty-Two

Kitty arrived at Sarah's Near North Side apartment a few minutes after midnight.

"Oh my gosh, Kitty. It's so good to see you. But why now? You mind telling me what the hell is going on?"

"The short version is that Patrick and I had a fight, and I wanted to leave. It was way too late to call Ross and Ann Hunter. You're a real lifesaver to let me spend the night."

They sat in her living room, which Sarah had recently redecorated with subtle beige wall covering, a new upholstered sofa and matching wing chairs. Kitty gingerly placed her damp tote bag on the new plush wool carpeting. "Your place looks great — quite a contrast with the old days, before I left here to stay with the Hunters."

"What happens now?"

"I need a breather from him, I'm hoping they'll take me back for a while."

"You're soaked and shivering. Why don't you take a hot shower and get ready for bed. You must be starved, and Buster is prowling around the kitchen as well."

Her friend made soup and a sandwich for her, gave Buster a bowl of water and a dish of leftovers, and made up the foldout couch in her living room. The food restored her physically and Sarah made her feel welcome. As they sat in her kitchen drinking herbal tea, she relaxed and told her tearful story. She began crying and couldn't stop.

"You poor dear! This must be tearing you apart. And pregnancy has made you blossom, prettier than ever."

"The worst of it is," Kitty said, "I was so excited about everything — our new baby, the house project and starting a new life. In a way I can't blame Patrick: Gloria kept it a secret when she left for Europe. But he has known this since she came back, and he still didn't tell me! Now I can hardly stand to look at him, and I'll never trust him again."

"Maybe things will seem better in the morning. Just lie down and go to sleep.."

She lay down on the sofa sleeper and allowed Buster to snuggle under the covers beside her. The herbal tea did its work, and she soon fell asleep.

◊

At eight in the morning Kitty called Ross and Ann Hunter's house and found Ann at home. She told her of the argument and rift with her new husband. Ann offered to take her in. Since Ross Hunter was on his way to work, she called his cell phone to re-route him.. He immediately picked her up and took her to their house. He explained that the law could not help the situation but was more concerned with her present feelings. He said she could stay as long as she wanted.

Sweet Ann Hunter steered away from sore subjects for the first few days and invited Kitty to putter with her in the garden. She turned her son's room over to her, now that he was away at college, made room in his closet for her few belongings and took her shopping in Winnetka's Elm Street for a couple of attractive maternity dresses.

Kitty had found a safe harbor in the storm.

Chapter Thirty-Three

The warm November day, tempered by a bracing breeze off the lake, inspired Gloria to set out on an excursion. Although she had her choice of suburban and exurban shopping malls north of the city, for old times' sake she decided to head downtown, scene of early memories of shopping trips with her mom. She guided her metallic burnt-orange Chevy Impala southward on I-94. Past farms and fields she rode, glancing right or left at grazing Guernsey cattle, iconic red barns with nearby pig pens, sheep pastures, horse corrals, contoured rows of winter wheat and stalks of nodding oats, framed against a background of purest blue sky dotted with puffy fair-weather clouds.

Since completion of the casino, her responsibilities had shifted from office and field supervision, which had only required jeans and office casual wear, to a more public presence. Since her mom was busy with her women's club activities, she'd planned a day of escape on a fanciful trip to indulge in some fine new fashions from her favorite stores: Saks Fifth

Avenue, Bonwit-Teller and the other stylish boutiques on North Michigan Avenue.

Retracing her old familiar route, she turned off the new I-94 highway near Peterson Avenue and headed due east — past shops, discount liquor stores, furniture clearance warehouses from an earlier era — to Sheridan Road, and turned south along the lake, passing the old Edgewater Beach Hotel and its cluster of mid-rise towers. At North Avenue Beach, a few intrepid swimmers plowed into the two-to-three-foot combers of a medium surf, while more timid souls clung to beach towels warming in the early afternoon sun. Belmont Harbor was alive with denim clad boaters as they prepared to set out. Various watercraft — cigarette boats, cabin cruisers and single masted sailboats — chugged under power to the mouth of the harbor.

Past this point the boulevard transitioned to Lake Shore Drive, lined with concrete lampposts alternating with Chicago's classic honey locust trees, which cast feathery shade on her car as she passed. Tall apartments of steel and glass towered on her right as she progressed southward toward downtown. As she coasted past they yielded to older mid-rise masonry structures, the old Gold Coast, where her grandparents had once lived.

Gloria reflected with pride on the recent progress she'd made to realize her personal and professional dreams. Endowed with her mother's inherited organizational skill and her father's ability to charm people, she fascinated the casino patrons and hotel guests. In the evenings she either taught patrons how to bet on the games or sat in the lobby and told stories of her travels, attracting groups of admirers. She engaged the staff as well and imparted to them an esprit de corps that inspired the whole team. Often, when she held an impromptu staff meeting, little Mike clung to her skirts, endearing them all the more to the lady in charge.

They saw her and Nick as the perfect couple, admired by her many fans. Gloria knew how to light up a room. Everyone wanted to do things for her. Glum staff members under her influence begin to see the bright side: they worked as a harmonious team. Guests spread the word about this wonderful place, distant and different enough from the daily grind to forget their troubles and enjoy a holiday.

Nick McGurk ran both his laundry businesses and casino operations with cool efficiency, From his long association with the Detroit mob, he resisted Jimmy Romo's efforts to horn in on his operations. He was on to Candicci's tricks and alerted Detective Sergeant O'Malley and Special FBI Agent Radwinski about any new suspicious activities. In a recent conversation, Romo threatened him again, and Nick hung up on him.

Instead of following the lakefront drive eastward around the north loop of apartment, office, and hospital buildings, she merged right near Oak Street Beach and headed straight south on Michigan Avenue. She drove almost to the Tribune Tower, parked on the lower level, below the elevated street, and climbed back up the steps to continue her shopping spree on foot.

With all this recent accomplishment to be proud of, Gloria couldn't understand why she felt such discontent. Although she was pleased with her success in getting the mob to release Kitty, she couldn't just relax and enjoy it. She told herself she bore no resentment toward Kitty for stealing Patrick. In many ways Kitty was better suited to Patrick's temperament than she had ever been. Gloria loved the limelight, money, clothes, the social scene, and getting to know large numbers of people. Patrick was more contemplative and inner-directed. He preferred quiet evenings at home, reading, watching his favorite television dramas and conversation with small groups of friends. Moreover, he was easily distracted by beautiful women, leaving her on edge about her status with him. Nick, with his admiration, sheer devotion, and constant wonder that he had won her love, had proven to be a far superior mate.

And yet despite all these logical reasons that should make her happy, Gloria had not expected to suffer so much over her loss. She thought she had always demonstrated her approval to Kitty and now hoped she might have clinched their friendship. Her own selfless act to defy her father and the outfit freed Kitty from the clutches of that foolish Candicci. Yet she could never feel totally at ease with her. It could not be Kitty's Irish heritage — it matched the national character of her father's Italian people: open, friendly and always talkative. Despite her father's generosity in sending her and her mother on a long postponed grand tour of Europe to forgive and forget, the real reasons behind her abrupt departure complicated her trip and curtailed her enjoyment. She didn't like to think about it and even now pushed it from her mind. But the feeling that Patrick should be with her persisted and rankled in her heart.

Gloria had always resented her father's mob activity. She cared for many things other than fame and fortune: nature, relationships, and good works, while she opposed evil motives and activities. Joe would never be fully free of the mob: the saying was, you could only retire feet first.. So it would be up to the women in the family to lash out, fight greed, corruption and crime, and suppress Chicago's shadowy underworld. She hoped to free her family and many others from the burden of its web, fulfill their potential, so they could live safe, prosperous, and happy lives. But she wondered if her dad could ever break free. Whenever Joe got close to putting it behind him, someone or something in the mob pulled him back in. It seemed hopeless.

She felt so lucky she'd found Nick and married him. He was not only undaunted by his stepfather role, he was also thrilled to be a parent. Welcoming a new member to the family so early in their marriage could not alter his love for Gloria. With the new life growing in her belly, they had become closer.

Nick had gone through a lot to win Gloria's trust. After securing his own escape from the Detroit mob, he had hung on to the small fortune he embezzled from them, invested wisely in a string of small businesses, and secured her rescue from capture by her father's own henchmen, ironically, in collaboration with Patrick. While Gloria was happy for her own good fortune, living her lifelong dream to escape, she also worried that Nick was doomed, like her father, to be sucked back into a criminal life.

Perhaps it was her secret that had kept the two women apart. Although she had openly shared it with Nick and he had accepted it lovingly, she wondered if Kitty suspected or even knew. But she didn't dare risk revealing it. It could disrupt and even ruin several lives.

Gloria got into the spirit of her shopping trip. At Saks she found a broad brimmed sun bonnet, a multicolored bikini and a frilly, filmy nightie — just the things to please and excite Nick. At Bonwit Teller she found a couple of sophisticated low-cut dresses, perfect for hosting their casino patrons, whom she tutored in gambling technique.

She descended the steps near the Tribune Tower to the lower level where she had parked her car. As she deposited her packages, closed the trunk, and prepared to leave, a woman parked her car in a nearby stall and approached her. She looked vaguely familiar.

"Hi Gloria, remember me?"

"Oh sure, from the hotel opening. What a nice article you wrote. It's Mona, right?"

"I was just going to get some lunch, and I do have some follow-up questions for you."

"Why not the back room at the Corona?" Gloria was hoping to benefit from their main restaurant's great main menu and the anonymity and discounted prices of the back room, low overhead diner.. "We could sit among the truck drivers and cabbies."

"It just recently closed."

"Oh, darn! Well, we could go right over here to the Billy Goat Tavern, unless you're worried about rival reporters."

"It's past lunch hour. There won't be many people there, anyway."

Gloria followed Mona Strong past more parked cars to the lower-level entrance of the iconic Billy Goat Tavern. She had forgotten that the tables had basic Formica tops with standard vinyl-seat metal tube chairs. The room's signature attraction was a strip of laminated newspaper clippings at eye level, documenting Chicago's most famous people, places, and memorable events. They sat in a far corner, away from the few late lunch customers.

"How have you been since I saw you at the groundbreaking?" Gloria said.

"Busy — the news never stops. But tell me, how is the hotel operation going?"

"Great! We're getting ready for our next big announcement—the formal opening of the casino next summer. We've planned a gala grand opening celebration, with a concert by the Corsairs at our open-air amphitheater. It's on the night before their big show at the United Center."

"Keep me posted. I'll be there!" She lowered her voice, "But tell me. How is Kitty doing after her ordeal?"

"She's doing fine, recovering with friends." Gloria had to be very careful here. She needed Mona's help in publicizing the casino but was aware that anything negative she might say about Patrick and Kitty's relationship could end up as sensational gossip in her column in the Tribune.

"She's not back together with Patrick?"

Gloria hesitated in her response. But unlike Mona, she could not be a convincing liar. A bit of lingering resentment over Kitty's success with Patrick — and the thought that she had left of her own accord and would have to account for it herself — prompted Gloria's reply.

"She needed time to recover, with friends in the suburbs."

"Oh, I see." She looked at her watch. "I've got to get back. Deadlines, you know. I'm so glad we bumped into each other. It was nice to have this chance to visit."

Before Gloria could even react, Mona grabbed the lunch check, paid the cashier and headed for her nearby office in the Tribune tower.

Chapter Thirty-Four

Detective O'Malley had called Patrick with his latest news. "Hensley Wilson's lawyer has made a detailed analysis of their client's occupancy dates, fingerprint evidence, and alibi. They proved that he could not have committed the murder.

"Bottom line: we don't have a case," O'Malley said. "We had to let him go."

"No problem. He'll be of more use to us trying to figure out how to renovate this house. Have you caught up with Candicci yet?" Patrick continued to play dumb at O'Malley's expense. "Jimmy Romo has scared him silly. He wants him to lay low back to Detroit."

"I hope he's out of town. He's caused enough trouble: your wife's kidnapping, as well as continued suspicion of the unsolved murder at the old house."

"I'll let you know if I find him around here."

Next Patrick called Nick McGurk, to inform him of the forensic findings and Hensley Wilson's exoneration.

"We may never find out who did it," Nick said.

"I'm not giving up yet," Patrick said.

"By the way, can you come out here early tomorrow? The local police chief wants to talk to me first thing. He says he has some new evidence, and you should hear it."

◊

At nine the next morning the two arrived at the police station on Rockville's main street. Although his modest office held mainly government issue metal furniture, Chief Roger Benson wore his full uniform and cut an impressive figure.

Nick introduced Patrick and explained his role in the project. "Since you both are involved in this investigation and know all the parties." Benson said, "I think you'll be interested in the information I've uncovered. I talked with Chicago police detective O'Malley and FBI agent Radwinski and about Detroit mobster Jimmy Romo's visit to Rockville,"

"As you know, Mr. McGurk, your wife invited me to inspect the hotel suite just after the Detroit mob boss left. My forensic expert swept Jimmy Romo's suite, gathered fingerprints and compared them with the sets of prints and other evidence Chicago police have already gathered on the suspects in the Chicago case.

"It turns out that some prints on the handle of the shovel match Romo's. Moreover, he is now a person of interest in the murder case. Our sheriff, however, who is up for reelection, is reluctant to release the information and involve other police departments. He wants to avoid the local embarrassment that he unknowingly sheltered this mob boss in his very own county. So I'm calling on you to connect the dots and inform these authorities. I'll invite them in to take over the case."

"I understand your position, Chief, and appreciate your help." They thanked him and and left the meeting.

They returned to the old farmhouse for lunch. Over sandwiches in the kitchen, Patrick acquainted Gloria with details of his break with Kitty.

"Oh Patrick, when I heard they had captured Kitty, I knew how complicated the situation was for you both. I am so sorry for my spiteful behavior on the house tour. I was out of line. When you talk to her, please let her know I was only trying to make sure you two would stay married and continue your new life together."

"I'll tell her when I can, but I doubt if mere words will help,"

Patrick and Nick then told her the police chief's conclusions about Romo in the murder case.

"What? Jimmy? Oh god no!"

"His fingerprint evidence from the hotel room," Nick said, "matched some of the prints on the shovel that killed Charles Simmons."

"That doesn't prove anything. It's not like him. When Pop was so busy he didn't have time for me himself, Jimmy was like a second father to me."

"You know how that goes," Nick said. "Business is business,"

"Sadly, I do." Tears filled her eyes. She excused herself and left the room.

158

Part III: Spirited Women

To hell with the likes of my warders, who I saw were Tito and Caesar Dellacroce. Let them do their worst, I told myself. And to hell with all the politicians on the take and the princes of industry who lionized Third World bedbugs in order to carry out their agenda of inculcating fear in the electorate at home. America was still America, the country everyone in the world wanted to emulate, where rock 'n' roll and the Beat lyrics of Jack Kerouac would outlive all the venal interests that threatened her.

—Dave Robicheaux in *Last Car to Elysian Fields,* by James Lee Burke, 2003

Chapter Thirty-Five

The days grew shorter, and the Hunters' long evenings moved indoors. Winter brought its first flurries of snow. Kitty settled into a routine — mornings working with Ann in the yard, cleaning around the house in the afternoons, and talking, reading, or watching favorite shows at night.

In these last golden days of fall, Kitty welcomed the opportunity to dig up bulbs for storage in the basement, prune fruit and hawthorn trees and help Ann groom their landscaped backyard for winter. She borrowed sweaters, sweatpants and jackets from their son's collection, donned work gloves and was content to spend many joyful hours outdoors. Much more at home than in their sterile glass cube above the city, both she and Buster flourished in the familiar outdoor scene. Framed by gold and red maples, tawny oaks and evergreen juniper hedges, both she and her loyal pet were in their element, forgetful of urban confinement, crime, and construction woes. And yet the signs of waning summer left her sad — Patrick wasn't there to share these magical moments.

She continued to benefit from the leave of absence caused by her unwilling captivity. Seamus and Lily granted her permission to stay with the Hunters as long as she needed, to recover before returning to work. She took advantage of her extra time to apply for conversion of the green card she had obtained when she began work at the pub to naturalized status. Once she had married Patrick, Hunter said she was now entitled to full citizenship it and needed to get the sluggish wheels of bureaucracy turning. Feeling guilty over their fight, she nonetheless completed her application based on her marital status.

One night after dinner they all sat down in the cozy den. "Whatever became of that fellow from Detroit?" Ross asked as he sipped his brandy. "The enforcer, who was a suspect in that downtown murder case."

"Oh, Candicci?" This drew out a more detailed history of her ordeal, which upset her more.

"My god!" Hunter said. "You told us about your recent kidnapping, but I didn't realize it was this Candicci. What a sick character. And he was never convicted as an accessory in the downtown murder?"

"Patrick said there wasn't enough evidence to implicate him directly."

"Where is he now?"

"He's still around, haunting that house we're trying to buy," Kitty said.

"This criminal needs to be put out of business. Who's handling the case?"

"Detective Sergeant. O'Malley — and I'm pretty sure the FBI is involved, an agent named Radwinski."

"Hmm, I've talked to O'Malley before. I'll give him a call tomorrow."

"Just don't tell him where I am. I'm perfectly happy here until Patrick comes to his senses."

◊

Kitty had been gone for days, and Patrick did not know where she was staying. When he read about it in the newspaper, he finally called her friend Sarah to see what she might know. She said she sheltered Kitty the night she disappeared. She knew only that she had left to stay with the family she had lived with before, but she couldn't remember the name. Patrick, of course, knew the number by heart and called the Hunters' house.

Ann Hunter answered, "Hello, Ann. Her friend Sarah tells me Kitty is staying with you for a while. May I speak to her?"

"I'll tell her, Patrick."

A couple of minutes later she returned. "She's here, but she doesn't want to talk to you."

"But this is terribly important. I want to apologize."

"It's going to take more than an apology, I'm afraid. Kitty is an emotional wreck. She's disillusioned and extremely unhappy with the direction things have taken. She's not ready to talk to you yet."

"But I don't understand. She seemed so excited about the new house and the renovation project. I thought she had calmed down and was convinced to stay until morning. But she went out in the storm to walk the dog and was gone. Is she alright? What's she doing?"

"Since you ask, she's in good health and very happy working with me outdoors in the garden, playing with the dog and, especially, thinking about things. Perhaps you should do some of that too."

"But I have been, very hard. I just don't understand it."

"When she ran off, there was your first clue, Patrick. It was raining in the middle of the night. Look what she had to do every day just to walk the dog! Have you really thought about your married life together? Why don't you call back in a couple of weeks? Maybe she'll be ready to talk then."

That evening with Ross and Kitty at dinner, Ann brought up Patrick's phone call. She resumed a conversation that had started the night Kitty arrived.

"You know," Ann said, "Gloria was trying to help you out by keeping her secret. Back then she didn't want to ruin your chances of marrying Patrick. She was really quite selfless,"

"Oh Ann, I know," Kitty replied. "But I can't forgive Patrick for fathering a child with her. Even when he found out, he still he kept it from me."

"Don't tell me you didn't take chances when you and Patrick fell in love. Accidents happen."

"Some nights I can't sleep because I've been so cruel to Patrick. But I don't know how to forgive him. Can we ever get back to our happy life?"

Ann got up from the table and brought in dessert — a fresh baked apple pie.

Except for expressing approval of her delicious dessert, they ate in silence, absorbed in their own thoughts.

"Kitty, it is what it is. You'll have to deal with it. If that's the worst fight you ever have in your marriage, you'll be doing better than most of us."

"I know. And Gloria is really much better suited to Nick. Patrick said so himself. Nick considers winning her love and helping raise the baby are the best things that ever happened to him. But still, how can I ever trust Patrick again and let him know how I feel?"

"How do you feel, Kitty. What is the real problem here?"

Anne gathered up their empty plates and made coffee.

Kitty helped her clean up the kitchen and they sat in the study. "For one thing, the more I learn about the sacrifices we'll have to make if we buy that house, the less I like it. It's a bad neighborhood. It won't be safe for our children to play in the yard or on the street. And it will take so much work and expense for us to get the house in livable condition. Compared with moving to St. Louis and — "

"What, you and Patrick are considering moving to St. Louis?" Ross asked.

"Well, yes. We took a weekend trip down there to see Mike and Rose. Patrick has a wonderful job waiting for him if we decide to go. We could build our own house, on a beautiful suburban lot. Patrick would design it just the way we both want it."

"It sounds to me like just what the doctor ordered," Hunter said. "It's a lovely town on the upswing, and it's a lot freer of entrenched corruption than this cursed city. If I were young enough to start over, I would gladly accept a situation like that."

"But I don't think he's seriously considering it. He has so many friends and good contacts here."

"That might be your answer," Ann said. "I think Patrick needs to start considering your needs and those of his future family as much as his own career. And in this case it seems he would sacrifice nothing. You should insist upon a big change like that — as a condition of your return."

A glint from the setting sun illuminated the room. An October breeze carried the sweet smell of autumn leaves, smoke and peonies into the study. They stood and moved to the back patio. Beyond the stately oaks of the backyard the sky glowed from pale blue to purple to orange. At last the fire-red disc of sunset disappeared behind the distant woods.

Kitty embraced Ross with one arm and Ann with the other and held them to her. "Oh, I love you both so much. You've helped me see my future, and now it looks so beautiful. I hope I'm not too late."

Chapter Thirty-Six

Kitty's first step in forgiving Patrick was to improve her understanding of him. There was no better source than Gloria. But how could she get out to the farmhouse? She figured Ann might enjoy a tour of the hotel casino site, and they made a plan to drive to Rockville. She checked with Gloria about her schedule. On the day she suggested, Kitty alighted at the farmhouse, while Nick conducted Ann on a tour of the new complex,

"It has been so long, and we have so much to catch up on," Gloria said. Once they were settled with their morning coffee in her cozy upstairs office, she started with a cheerful topic. "How was your trip to see Patrick's aunt and uncle?"

"St. Louis is a lovely place. Patrick's Uncle Mike and Aunt Rose were great hosts. They live in a wooded valley subdivision a half-hour from downtown, with a creek, hills and lots of beautiful trees."

"It sounds very nice. I've never been there," she said in a dismissive tone.

"We also met lots of interesting people. Mike's St. Louis architectural consultant has a downtown office with a view of the arch."

"I'm so glad you were able to get away after your horrible ordeal. I don't know how much you know about it. But behind the scenes I put the screws to that ridiculous Candicci and got him to toe the line."

"Patrick told me all about it. Thank you so much! I did what I could to get him to buy some decent food and behave, but his incessant smoking and that ranting TV channel were driving me crazy."

"We haven't seen him lately. Jimmy Romo wants him to lay low, back in Detroit."

"That would be good riddance, indeed!"

"While you were gone I thought a lot about you and Patrick. I knew that man intimately. I always hoped his physical attraction to me would deepen into true love. But it never happened."

"I've never really understood it either. You're so perfect in every way One would think he'd never get enough of you."

"Physical beauty is a blessing and a curse. For me, men are easy to attract, but the really good ones are so hard to keep."

"But you have both beauty and brains."

"I'm not sure it's enough," she said, but her mind was racing ahead. She and Patrick were still not reconciled after their fight. She wanted to forgive him but was still struggling to understand her own emotions. What was keeping her from fully forgiving Patrick?

"You have more important attractions. You understand him and can love him in a way I never could." She stood and reached for Kitty. "Come, here, my dear."

Gloria encircled her tightly. Almost a head taller, with Kitty's head cradled on her breast, her torso hugged Gloria's flat stomach and thighs

Kitty's ear touched something small on a chain, Drawing away she admired a diamond teardrop pendant. "Oh, how beautiful!"

"Yes, Seamus gave it to Lily when their pub began to succeed. She proudly gave it to me to bless our future marriage. Patrick loved to see me wear it."

"I'm surprised you never wear it in public. It's so pretty,"

"I can't bear to hurt Nick's feelings. I shouldn't really hang on to it any longer. You have won him — it rightly belongs on you. She removed it and gently draped it around Kitty's neck. They embraced, more tenderly and closely than before. Gloria whispered in her ear, "You've allowed me to let go. From now on, you'll carry the torch of love for Patrick."

Whether it was the long-denied press of another body or the spirit of Patrick in the teardrop talisman, Kitty's heart beat faster. The heat of desire rose in her loins, and she craved Patrick's kiss. Somehow Gloria's body had rekindled in her own the hunger for her husband's touch, her unslaked thirst for his love. Breathless, she released her grip and stared into her friend's liquid brown eyes,

"Oh, Gloria, thank you from the bottom of my heart!"

The next morning, Kitty gathered her courage and called Patrick on his cell phone. There was no answer. She couldn't bear to leave a message.

Chapter Thirty-Seven

Patrick wanted to call Kitty but, so often rebuffed, didn't even try. Hensley Wilson had agreed to release the couple from the sale contract, based on multiple inspections and required repairs that would greatly reduce the sale price. Patrick mailed the official notification letter with a copy of Chet's report and drove toward Bond Street. He wanted a last look at what might have been.

From outside, the house had a sullen, deserted air. Rather than promise for the future, it spoke to him of foreboding horror. For the first time he noticed the tower was not fully aligned with the façade —why? He saw that the side property line and the driveway along it made a slightly acute angle with the street. To avoid its jutting into the driveway, the architect for the tower addition rotated its square base slightly to parallel the driveway.

Inside, dust covers still draped the living room chandeliers, and the same shadows shrouded the uppermost regions of the cavernous rooms. On the master bedroom wall, the two dour ancestors of its builders still stared disapprovingly from their perch.

Moreover, the empty house still transmitted thumping and creaking sounds from above. At first he shook his head and muttered, "Maybe Kitty was right — it is haunted, if from nothing else, by rotten luck."

He toured the bedrooms and made a last appraisal, which he tried to keep objective, of the beautiful woodwork, but also the obvious cracks and multiple flaws that cried out for correction. He shook his head in resignation — the shortcomings clearly outnumbered the benefits.

The sounds from above had fallen silent, but now he heard a muffled hiss on the third floor above. He checked the closet, smelled smoke. and dashed up the tower steps to the hidden attic bedroom. A fire smoldered at the base of the big armchair, the only light in the darkened space. Coughing and gasping for air, he charged through the fumes toward the slumping Marco Candicci, about to be overcome with smoke. Patrick grabbed the throw rug, yanked down the curtains, and threw them on top of the smoldering mass, in an attempt to smother the fire.

"Candicci, Wake up!" Patrick yelled.

The man awoke, looked around and muttered, "Oh crap, I must've fallen asleep — good catch." He lifted the overturned ashtray from the floor and stood. "I have to show you something." He led Patrick to the basement wine cellar, where the ornate chess table still sat at the rear of the narrow space. Yet now, one chair was tipped over. Chessmen lay scattered in disarray on the floor. A nearly empty bottle of the treasured Châteauneuf du Pape stood in its center, next to an empty glass. "Last night, he said, "the ghost of Charles Simpson challenged me to a chess match."

"I don't see your glass." Patrick said.

"I abstained from drinking, as is my habit, these last dozen years."

"What happened?"

"I wagered my soul against absolution from his murder."

"So, it was you!" Patrick said. "But how is this killing so different from all your other hits."

"Then I was merely following orders, for the good of the family — that was my job. I admitted to Simpson I was wrong, but I've been haunted ever since.

"But Simpson's murder was wrong," Patrick said. "He was merely defending his rightful home."

"Precisely," Candicci said. "That was his reaction. He insisted we play for my salvation. I lost."

"He said his spirit will never rest until I am destroyed. I will never be free from my guilt at the innocent man's death."

"Oh, come on, Marco," Patrick asserted, "you don't really believe in this spook nonsense, do you? You've got something to live for. Cool off, do what Jimmy Roma wants, you do your time, and you'll be useful and happy again."

"It's not that simple."

"I'll drink to that for both of us." Patrick grasped the bottle, which still held two fingers of the precious spirits. He lifted it to his lips and sipped. The wine had not turned and indeed still held its good structure, smoky aroma, and robust flavor, as he recalled it from the recent tasting.

"It is as fine as the wine I drank the other day," he declared to Candicci. "Proof enough that the being you saw was just a figment of an overactive mind."

The thug gazed on in baffled wonder. Then his eyes widened in horror, and he raised his arm. "Look there, he returns!"

Patrick saw nothing new where he pointed. But the chess table rocked as if struck from behind. Then, with an evident strong shove, it careened toward them, balanced an instant on its far edge and crashed on its side, breaking the bottle and scattering more chessmen on the rocky floor.

With a guttural roar, Candicci rose, turned, and raced toward the stairway. Eager to pursue but frightened to his core, Patrick was no less intent on escaping from this phantom ghoul.

He chased the gangster up the main stairs to the attic.

Candicci glanced back over his shoulder and paused.

"What the hell are you doing in this house?" Patrick demanded.

"You think you control everything," he shouted, barely audible over crackling of the fire, "gloating over poor bastards like me, just struggling to do my job."

"Hardly! What keeps you hiding out here, causing trouble?"

Flames licked the closet by the tower. The heat increased a notch; the sound rose to a roar.

"You invaded my space," the mobster said. "First, you had the beautiful Gloria. Now it's, that she-devil Kitty. I had her in my clutches, but she got to me. Watch out she doesn't take control of you!"

"Aha, you 're jealous! So that's why you won't leave us alone."

"Besides, you've muscled me out of the casino. Now Jimmy thinks I'm useless and wants me out of circulation."

"You tried to muscle in — and failed. He doesn't trust you to handle a simple hit job."

"I hit him, alright. That meddling owner was in my way, blocked me at every turn, I took care of that."

Facing the closed door to his chamber, Candicci dove straight at it, shattering the frame. Black smoke poured past him into the hallway. Inside, it had engulfed his chair. The main stair was blocked by his onrushing pursuer.

Flames now licked the closet. Smoke drifted into the tower enclosure. He scrambled through the only exit left the closet, to the tower stairs. Smoke drifted upward from below, and appeared to block escape. Instead, he raced upward toward the cupola. Patrick pursued him up the stairs, yelling, "Not that way, you idiot, you'll never get out!" Candicci turned and resumed his climb.

Patrick followed him, five steps behind.

"Marco, come down here with me. You have a long life ahead of you."

"Yeah sure, in a padded cell. I'll take my chances with the devil," He broke into a fit of coughing and climbed again as thicker smoke rose in the narrow shaft.

"Candicci, you fool. Come back here!" He pursued him up the steps and tried to catch him. But he was out of reach. Patrick climbed on doggedly Puffing and coughing, he stopped and stared. Candicci crashed through a cupola window and plunged to the driveway below.

Frosty, fresh air gushed in through the wrecked sash opening. Patrick paused for a moment, took one last deep breath, and rushed downward through the flames. He landed painfully, turning his ankle, at the opening to the smoky interior. He limped down the tower stairway toward the vestibule exit and safety.

The fire above had now involved most of the mansard attic and a large portion of the roof. Instead of clear air below, he felt a hot updraft. Black smoke poured upward toward him, thickening as he watched. Firemens' shouts reached him from the shaft below. He paused to rest his throbbing ankle. His architect's brain raced to understand. Something was terribly wrong.

Crap. In a flash He knew why.

The heavy black smoke from the roof was flooding the spacious main stairwell. Fire crews had left the tower door open, admitting this smoke to the tower shaft. The minute Candicci plunged though the window, the rising hot air had found an exit and created a chimney effect in the tower. Both his escape on the main stairway and retreat down the tower steps were now blocked by thick, deadly fumes. Patrick was trapped.

He took a last deep breath, held it and descended through rising smoke to the second-floor level. His only hope was a double stained-glass window on the opposite face of the tower. He sprang down the steps to reach it and landed. His injured left leg collapsed in excruciating pain, Patrick was seized by a fit of coughing. His eyes dimmed. He gathered his failing strength, straightened, and kicked with his good leg at the vertical mullion between the two panes of leaded glass. His other knee collapsed and left him painfully straddling the jagged glass of the opening, with his right leg outside. He thrust his torso through the broken sash and inhaled the chilly air in desperate gasps.

"Help," he croaked with his last breath and slumped in the opening.

◊

Neighbors had reported the fire, The first pumper to arrive had connected to a hydrant and poured streams of water toward the blaze, which now engulfed the whole attic floor.

A fireman spotted a figure in the tower window and shouted, 'Hey, that survivor has just collapsed. Get the rescue vehicle over here, pronto."

A huge firefighter with an asbestos suit and breathing tanks placed a tall ladder against the tower and labored up toward the figure in the window. He gently threaded his victim the rest of the way out, slipped an oxygen mask over his face and slung the heavy inert form over his shoulder as he backed down the ladder. The huge fireman placed him gently on the side driveway pavement, then squatted between Candicci's body and Patrick's reclining form.. He removed his own mask and surveyed the scene, wheezing from his exertion and attempting to recover.

The first fireman took over resuscitation efforts. Soon Patrick was breathing on his own. His eyes fluttered open. The mobster lay where he had landed, in a pool of blood from every opening, his body still, his limbs sprawled in contorted, unnatural positions. The bleeding had stopped

The firefighter grilled Patrick, "Anybody else in there?"

"No, I was the last," he said through his dim perception and pain. "I tried to save Candicci, but the idiot jumped from up there anyway." Gagged by a coughing spell, he pointed weakly toward the cupola with its gaping, broken window sash.

Sparks flew wildly, igniting wood roof shingles to an unearthly orange. Against the twilight sky, cast iron cresting glowed in white-hot profile. Soon the entire cupola was enveloped in flame. A tower of black fumes rose, marking the site. Attracted like bees to the hive, other fire companies clogged the narrow street, already littered with snaking hoses, into immobility.

Candicci had attached himself to this haunted site and might now haunt it forever. The spiraling smoke carried his soul on a long, dreary climb to salvation in an upward purgatory from the lowest circle of hell.

The fireman shouted to the man on the ladder, "Give it up, there's no one left to save!" Strapped to a gurney with his ankle iced, Patrick breathed easier as they slid him into the back of the waiting rescue van. He closed his eyes in utter exhaustion.

Chapter Thirty-Eight

The next morning Chet answered the phone in his office. It was O'Malley.

"Hey, Noo-zing, got some good news for you for a change. Your buddy Patrick survived the fire at the Victorian house last night."

"My god," I just heard about the fire on the morning news. "How is he? Where is he?"

"He's at St. Luke's Hospital. He can sit up and talk this morning. A few burns, scratches, some smoke inhalation, and he broke his ankle. Other than that, he's fine. Candicci didn't make it, jumped out of a goddamned window — that's the best news, as far as I'm concerned."

"Candicci is dead? I can't believe it!"

"Yep, saves us a lot of trouble. That cursed house was badly damaged by fire. When I saw him earlier, Patrick was almost back to normal, his usual annoying self."

"Thanks for the heads up. We'll talk more later."

He sat stunned, unable to focus, his mind awhirl with consequences, changed circumstances, and things he must do immediately.

His next call was to break the news to Kitty and the Hunters, who demanded to know where Patrick was taken. He told Ross what he knew, and they planned to drive with Kitty to see him. He stuffed his briefcase with his phone messages, a couple of memos and some of his work files and headed for his car.

The duty nurse on his floor said he could visit him, but only briefly. He had an appointment with the orthopedist in half an hour to diagnose and treat his ankle. He found him sitting up with his foot iced and elevated, finishing his breakfast. Chet had a barrage of questions ready.

"What have you done to yourself? And what went on in that house yesterday?"

Patrick ate with a fierce appetite. Between bites of scrambled eggs, toast and sips of coffee, he gave his friend the short version of his ordeal.

"Man, sorry!" Chet said, "That house was truly cursed."

"I've been thinking a lot since Kitty's been gone. I realized at last she was only going along with the project to please me. In fact, that house didn't suit her in almost any way. In the morning, I sent our contract release with your report. But I went in there for one last look."

"And Candicci was there?"

"Yeah, it seems that's where he went when he disappeared. He was somehow attached to that property and spent a lot of time in that attic bedroom. He fell asleep smoking in his chair. That tinder-dry wood caught almost immediately. He ran for the main stairway, but I was standing there. I tried to lead him down the tower stairs, but he headed for the roof. When I chased him up the cupola and tried to grab him, he jumped from the highest point of the tower. I probably caused his death."

"Like hell you did! You tried to save his life. He had no business smoking in there, he was trespassing, and after all, he kidnapped your wife and might have killed her."

"I guess you're right." He shook his head. "That damned house haunted me. Kitty and I were almost stuck with it. The whole thing was insane — the wrong place to start a family."

"Take it slowly, Patrick. You're alive, she's safe, and she'll be here to see you soon."

They chatted until the orthopedist's nurse appeared at the door with a wheelchair. It was time for Chet to leave. He gave him his phone memos, a couple of files, and items he had to read and respond to and left the building.

Chapter Thirty-Nine

The Hunters and Kitty arrived at the hospital while Patrick was with the orthopedist. In the austere waiting room, Ross fidgeted and checked his e-mail, Ann busied herself with her knitting and kept one eye on Kitty for signs of stress.

Kitty reflected on their estrangement and her regret at losing contact with Patrick. She tried to assume the proper balance between sympathy and setting new conditions. For days she had been preparing a speech for the moment he called. On the one hand, she would beg forgiveness. On the other she would express her doubts. She would protest all the flaws of that Victorian wreck as a future home: a bad neighborhood, never-ending construction on this money pit, and the haunting memory of crimes on that street. This would be a terrible place to raise a family. "Forget your architectural museum," she would declare. And she could no longer stand living in the grim ice cube of the lakefront apartment either, with its wintry seascape, the absence of fresh air, and a total lack of accessible outdoor space.

Now what could she say? Once the house had been destroyed by a five-alarm fire and Patrick almost killed, everything was changed. Her conversations with Ann and Ross evoked her true feelings about the situation. Her visit with Gloria blessed their marriage and rekindled her desire. But before she could accept a reunion, she had to set some ground rules. Finally, she spoke.

"Ann, I hope I can get through this without falling apart. I'm so worried about my future with Patrick, but so glad he survived. How can I tell him what he needs to know?"

"Your main duty is to listen." Ann carefully knitted and purled her stitches without looking up but kept talking. "You don't need to be cold-hearted. There will be plenty of time to say the rest." They fell into a companionable silence, broken only by periodic calls for doctors on the hall intercom and the click of knitting needles. Presently the duty nurse appeared in the door.

"He's back in his room now." She led the way to his double room, where the other occupant snoozed behind a curtain. Kitty took the seat next to the window by his bed, while Ann occupied the faux-leather armchair in the corner, and Hunter stood against the far wall. Patrick was sitting up, his ankle wrapped and propped, with a bandage across his forehead. His face looked curiously bare — his eyebrows had been singed off.

"Patrick, you look like a ghost!" When she saw him in this condition, her heart melted. She forgave him instantly and completely. She held him gently by the shoulders and kissed him on a freshly shaved cheek.

"Almost happened, and I saw one. But I'm still painfully alive."

"See, I thought so! What did it look like?"

"It had an uncanny resemblance to Marco Candicci — in fact, he couldn't leave the place and fell asleep smoking."

"I know — I saw the report on the news. That was our house! Now what?"

"Enough about that. Kitty. I am so sorry about our misunderstanding. I've been a bad, thoughtless husband. I haven't been thinking about you, your happiness, nor our family. And I've given a lot of thought to my future prospects. I'm not sure Chicago is the place for our kids to grow up, nor the best place for me. Uncle Mike's vision sounds more attractive every day."

"You mean — we really might go?" Her prepared speech, rendered useless, flew from her mind.

"Only if that's what you want, Kitty."

"Oh, I've thought about it too: I want to live away from all this urban crime, amidst nature, in a home we have designed together in a beautiful spot. It should have places for our children to play, a yard to get outside in the nice weather and plenty of space to entertain our guests — and no restoration projects!"

"It would be possible, if we take Uncle Mike's proposal seriously. That's what we could do next — accept my new job and make other plans."

"Oh, how wonderful! But what about this mess of a house we're leaving behind?"

"I saw it would never be a home for you, nor even for my so-called career. For less trouble and expense, we could start from scratch and build a new one of our own design. Hensley Wilson agreed to our withdrawal from the contract. Yesterday morning I rejected the contract, enclosed Chet's detailed report and put it in the mail. He should have received it this morning."

"Still, I feel bad for Hensley Wilson — now he is stuck with it."

"Not really. You'll see."

The duty nurse rushed into the room. "Mr. MacKenna, there is someone her to see you. He's not a relative or friend."

"Who is it?

"He's from the sheriff's office. He was very insistent. May I let him in?"

Hunter stepped forward. "You can't stop him. He's a law officer."

An official looking officer entered. Although there was a chair available, he remained standing. "Mr. MacKenna. We need to ask you some questions."

"My wife and I were just celebrating my survival. Can't this wait?"

"Sorry for your condition, sir. But I'm under orders to interview you now."

As the officer moved toward the bed. Kitty stood aside and sat on the arm of the corner chair next to Ann. "I told the fire officials what happened. Don't you have their report?"

"We do, sir. But we still find you are a person of interest the death of Marco Candicci."

"What could possibly be the problem?" Patrick said.

"You were the last person to see him alive. He had been harassing you. One fireman said you told him you chased him up the stairs."

"He chose to run up toward the cupola instead of down the stairs to safety. I told him it was the wrong way and chased him, to try to save his life. Before I got there, he jumped."

"Yes, we have your testimony from the report. You had previously threatened Candicci."

"You're damned right I did. That bastard kidnapped my wi-i-fe!" His voice failed in a coughing fit.

"You had the motive, the means and the opportunity at hand to silence him. And your violent temper is a matter of police record. "Who's to say you didn't push him?"

"Idle speculation, officer." Hunter stepped forward to confront the cop. "What exactly is your jurisdiction in this matter?"

"I was asked to look into this man's questionable conduct by the sheriff in Rockville."

"Deputy, my name is Ross Hunter, attorney and member of the Illinois bar. Mr. MacKenna cannot and will not make any response to your hearsay evidence without a formal charge. Furthermore, this matter is officially out of your jurisdiction. Take it up with Detective Sergeant O'Malley of the Chicago Police and Special Agent Radwinski of the FBI."

Kitty, who had been listening wide-eyed, dashed into the hallway. She returned with the duty nurse. "Sir, you are upsetting and destabilizing my patient. I'm going to have to ask you to leave."

"The nurse is within her rights," Hunter added. "You may leave now."

Chapter Forty

Architects are normally serious, due to their great responsibility for public safety, building performance, and beauty in our built environment. But they also enjoy making jokes — both on their buildings, such as fanciful finials, grotesque statues of their bosses on roofs, and modern-day gargoyles — and another type, "in" jokes about their own architectural practice.

Chet encountered such an inside joke when he first unrolled prints of the original plans for their new space in the downtown office building. He was ready to begin laying out the company's new tenancy for a full floor of this building. Since the building was narrow and wide, the floor plan had been split into two halves. On the west half of the floor, a small room at the center was only half shown, with side walls extending beyond the break line separating the two halves. He assumed that the door to the room would be found on the other half sheet. When he turned to that page, no door was shown. Two different draftsmen had assumed the other guy would take care of it and show a door on the drawings. This hidden, unused enclosure, finally discovered years later, had become an office joke.

When he went to the building and entered the vacant office floor to check existing conditions, he found that a door had been added and labeled, Telephone Room. In the early days of the last century, the complex circuits needed for a large office were handled by banks of switching equipment in what was called a frame room. Sometime in the 1930s, the phone system installers found and made use of this unclaimed space for the switching equipment for the office system. Since then, modern microelectronics had miniaturized these requirements, accommodating all these complex operations on printed computer circuit boards within a small wall cabinet. In this office the change was made sometime in the 1960s, leaving the room vacant again.

Chet consulted Patrick, and they decided to dedicate this room as a special space as a library and conference space, apart from the office collection of product catalogs and specification files. He called the Sit Room — a sitting or situation room for urgent or confidential office meetings of the firm's principals. They added new wall coverings, comfortable conference furniture and some handsome bookshelves for the firm's collection of business, management, and law books, as well as a "wisdom shelf," with some of their favorite fiction and nonfiction volumes, by such authors as James Michener, Doris Kearns Goodwin, Kurt Vonnegut, Ernest Hemingway, T. S. Eliot and Mark Twain. They left the sign denoting the room's original function unchanged — still true, as the location of telephone switching equipment.

On Patrick's first day back at the office Jason Holdroyd encouraged him to take it easy and not worry about getting work done, and to leave early if he got tired. He spent a couple of hours catching up with phone messages and digging into the pile of accumulated matters cluttering his desk. At noon, Chet stuck his head into his office. "Listen, buddy, you can't walk to our neighborhood bar, but we sure need to talk." Today, with Patrick's infirmity, they needed an emergency substitute for the scene of deep discussions at the Cloistered Oyster bar, which was now a few more blocks away.

They both had brought lunches and made their way slowly over to the telephone room. Most employees were out for lunch or in the break room, and no one noticed when Chet pulled out his key and they went in. He found what he was looking for on the wisdom shelf, pulled out a book with a yellow front cover, and began turning its yellowed pages.

"This is my dad's 1976 first edition of Slapstick, signed by the author Kurt Vonnegut, Jr. In his own brilliantly analytical and hilariously funny way, he explained what's been going on in our country for the past half-century."

"I got the paperback when they reprinted it a few years ago." Patrick said. "There's a lot of wisdom in there. It seems especially relevant today, to think this is where we've come. It's kind of sad, very funny and philosophical. But it closes the loop on what we can do about it."

"I need his wisdom on America today. Dad was a product of the 60s — the era of sacvastic comedians Mort Sahl, Lenny Bruce and Dick Gregory. This was his Bible when it first came out."

They took seats at the conference table and began eating. Patrick poured some iced tea into the cup of his thermos and Chet drank a can of soda from the machine.

"Dad was a baby boomer — too straight to be a hippie — but he tried, with his long sideburns, octagonal glasses and bell-bottom pants. He looked up to his dad as a member of the Greatest Generation. He had fought in World War II, against the Nazi menace, back when they all knew what they were fighting for and agreed on the truth.

"Here's one of my favorite lines from Slapstick:

> Yes, and Indianapolis, which had once had a way of speaking all its own, and jokes and legends and poets and villains and heroes all its own and galleries for its own artists, itself became an interchangeable part of the American machine.

"In Dad's day, Chicago was like that: they had Al Capone, Studs Terkel, Colonel Robert R. McCormick and his Tribune, Mike Royko from the Daily News, Joe Louis, the champion boxer who opened his own dairy, and Martha Roundtree, original moderator of the show that became Meet the Press."

"Really? Today, we have the network broadcasts, and even the farmers and ranchers in rural areas get the same shows."

"Back then most radio shows originated from Chicago," Chet said, "which is the reason the neutral, clearly articulated Midwestern accent became the broadcast standard for the media."

"True, but where are you going with this?"

"Vonnegut looked at the power structure with an objective eye, casually nailing the heart of the matter when introducing his characters, as if everyone already knew it:

> Our parents were silly and pretty and very young people named Caleb Mellon Swain and Leticia Vanderbilt Swain, née Rockefeller. They were fabulously well-to-do, and descended from Americans who had all but wrecked the planet with a form of Idiot's Delight — obsessively turning money into power, and then power back into money again, and then money back into power again."

"I see what you mean. He explains what went on then. His commentary doesn't seem dated — it is going on to an even greater degree today, more openly than ever."

"Right, and the two main characters in the parable describe themselves as children and explain their point of view" He read:

> This person has just arrived on this planet, knows nothing about it, has no standards by which to judge it. This person does not care what it becomes. It is easier to become absolutely anything it is supposed to be. . . . And all of the information we received about the planet we were on indicated that idiots were lovely things to be.
>
> So we cultivated idiocy.
>
> We refused to speak coherently in public, ... 'Buh,' and, 'Duh,' we said. We drooled and rolled our eyes. We ate library paste.
>
> "Their parents' army of child-rearing experts concluded that the two children were born mentally challenged and were likely to remain so. As wealthy and conscientious parents, they moved them to a rich uncle's remote mansion on a mountaintop, with servants and caretakers to provide them with everything they needed or desired. The two children kept their secret until they came of age. Meanwhile they had read every book in the mansion's well stocked library and discovered that, when they were together, their minds functioned on the genius level. The wicked irony of the parable is that many people in our society are happy to continue their easily fulfilled roles in the economy and just have fun. They are more than

willing to vote for someone who tells them what to do and what to think, so they don't have bother with the hard work of democracy, which requires them to think for themselves."

"That's brilliant! No wonder you're so impressed," Patrick said. "It fully explains frustration of the rest of us in a democracy today, who feel helpless to understand why so many people would rather live under a dictator."

"Those carefree types," Patrick continued, "would rather enjoy their freedom and live their lives. Yet they would remain in blissful ignorance of their debt to those who had sacrificed or died in wars to preserve our collective liberty. Those heroes fought against oppression and tyranny and for our right to free expression and self-determination. They also defended the rights of all people, regardless of race, creed, or national origin. As a result we could all enjoy the heritage of those heroes, like your dad. of that Greatest Generation, and many generations before them, back to two world wars, the Civil War, and the revolution against the British tyranny that led to the new nation's birth. But it raises the question: is democracy dying?"

"Oh, we might elect a few more presidents before the carefree squanderers of liberty wake up." Chet followed Patrick's train of thought and picked it up without a hitch. "By then they will and realize we've not only lost our own rights, but we have also abandoned leadership of the free world."

"Kurt Vonnegut's dire prophecy could really come true." Patrick said. "In this book wealthy entrepreneurs like Stewart Rawlings Mott, the apple tycoon, could become King of Michigan. Someone like the hundred-year-old King of Manhattan and last president of the United States, Wilbur Swain, would be in charge — of nothing, because by then, due to dismantling of the public health agencies and resulting plagues, no one remained in the government for him to direct, And as in the parable, there would very few people left to govern.

"But it's happening, here in Chicago, and everywhere else. Sadly, Vonnegut's vision makes sense."

"Before our very eyes," Patrick said, "and it's unlikely to be reversed. We have done our civic duty: we voted for our candidates, fought for our beliefs, and defended our arguments. We'll continue our fight But our counsel falls on deaf ears of the increasingly large percentage of people who are busy enjoying their remaining "freedom," while their liberty is dwindling and could soon be gone!"

To the logical minds of Patrick and Chet this realization closed the loop. It was a devastating conclusion, but it was the only possible way to understand what was happening and retain their sanity.

"But that wasn't the end of their story," Chet continued. "When Wilbur and Eliza put their heads together (literally touching, side by side), their combined mental capacity was on the genius level. They realized that the biggest problem of isolated members of an outward, media-focused society was that they were lonesome. Their greatest remedy and invention was a system of randomly assigning new middle names to every person in America. A byproduct of this effort was that it formed artificial families, of those sharing the same middle name, and created a common interest in each other's rights, interests, and well-being. Discussing an inscription over the entry to a building, Wilbur says:

> So many crimes are committed by lonesome people in Government are concealed in this place….that the inscription might well read, :'Better a family of criminals than no family at all.'

"Formation of these groups had the tendency to override conflicts and differences thaw normally occur among complete strangers: It was impossible to incite fights among the groups, because someone always had a brother, sister or cousin with the same middle name, who demanded that their 'relative' be tolerated because of the members' fierce loyalty to their groups. 'Because we're just families and not a nation anymore' they reasoned. 'it's much easier for us to give and receive mercy in war.'"

"Interesting, but Vonnegut made these observations when the book was first published in 1976," Patrick noted. "Since the internet was invented, Facebook, Twitter and other networks link people who have common interests — people from the same place, bird lovers, hockey fans, members of the same profession and other categories. These 'families' are the modern equivalent of Vonnegut's idea about common middle names"

"Back then, no one had ever heard of Facebook or Twitter, what we call social networking today."

"True," Chet said, consulting the yellow book, "it's right here." When asked to speak to a convention of his own middle-name group, Wilbur explained what he felt was his greatest achievement as the last President of the United States:

> "I would have liked to give my country peace as well as brotherhood and sisterhood. … There is no peace, I'm sorry to say. We find it. We lose it. We find it again. We lose it again. Thank God, at least, that the machines have decided not to fight anymore. It's just people now."

"Do you remember those Greek statues of old men, with worn faces and haunted eyes?" Chet asked.

"Yes — through the hands of these skilled sculptors I felt I was looking at their actual eyes and seeing into their despairing souls. They knew what others could only guess — the golden age of democracy in Athens was gone."

"Now there is nothing more we can do: Reagan's shining city on the hill has lost its luster. Short of a new miracle, the beacon of liberty will be dead."

"But we're not old men," Chet said. "Like Vonnegut's idols, Stan Laurel and Oliver Hardy, let's keep trying to improve the things we can change. We should keep reasserting our democratic ideals in the face of lying, power-hungry politicians through our actions. We have to pin our hopes for the future on that!"

Chapter Forty-One

The next morning, Jimmy Romo appeared at the farmhouse just as Gloria was about to go upstairs to work. She greeted him at the door.

"My gosh, Uncle Jimmy, back in town so soon?"

"Never left," he said. "Now, with the news of his death, I no longer have to hang around and babysit Marco. So sad, I had such hopes for him."

"What was wrong with that guy? Couldn't you keep him in line?"

"He wasn't useless, but he had a conscience, which he was working through. It was sad to lose him that way."

Gloria led him into the kitchen. Nick was refilling his coffee cup to take up to his office.

"Morning, Jimmy," he said over his shoulder, "want coffee?".

"Hi Nick. Sure."

"I was part of Candicci's problem," Nick said. "He felt left out. But I couldn't afford to allow him to attend our meetings."

"He had woman problems," Jimmy continued. "He could command his troops all right, but you and Kitty got under his skin. When he kidnapped her, she also began to work on him. His conscience wouldn't leave him alone."

Gloria invited him to sit at the table and set his cup of black coffee and a bowl of sugar in front of him. He took a jelly doughnut from the open box sitting in the middle of the table.

"After he kidnapped her, she started talking, asking him questions and wouldn't shut up. She made him feel guilty about kidnapping her, mistreating women and trying to end her happy marriage. Then she dropped the bombshell that she was pregnant. She had him so tied in knots, all he could do was confess his sins and hope for her absolution. After he delivered his hostage to you, he couldn't stay away from the house and literally haunted it. He spied on Kitty and Patrick. Maybe he fell in love with her — maybe he wanted her to be in his life but knew he could never have someone like her."

"Jimmy, I never did figure out why you were so worried about Marco. Why are you taking it so hard?"

"I'd rather not talk about it."

"Come on, Jimmy—this is more than support of a wayward employee. With someone like that on my staff, I would have given up on him a long time ago."

"Let's put it this way: you and Patrick would do anything in the world to help little Mike, right?"

"Of course, but— Oh my god! I get it." Gloria got up from the table and ran to the window, and Nick followed.

Morning sunbeams dispersed the mist over the lake, casting rays through the cloud to the water, where a gaggle of geese covered a large area. resting from their toil. Something told the leaders of the pack to leave, and they took off, followed in military formation by a widening column of flapping wings. to resume the season's southward trip. Gloria identified with these fowl. They had a mission — and no pain, nor storm. nor sheer adversity could deter them from their flight.

Nick turned and rejoined the group. "So that's what my problem has been all these years!" Nick said. "Always losing out to Marco — the favorite, the trusted, the chosen one. They talked quietly and both turned and surrounded Roma. "Jimmy," Gloria said, "we're so sorry. This must be the end of the world for you."

"If Maria could see this, if she were not already dead, this would kill her."

"When Maria died in that raid on your office ten years ago — I figured she might have been Marco's mother. But you, his dad? I don't understand."

"She married James Candicci — that's me. When her family threatened to disown her if she married a murderer, I changed my name, so when we met she could pretend Jimmy Roma was somebody new."

"I'm truly sorry for your loss Jimmy," Nick said. "I can't imagine how you must feel."

"Don't beat yourself up over it, kid. I owe you. I should have tried harder to make a spot for you. It didn't happen. Maybe the best thing I can do for you now is to go quietly back to Detroit and leave you and Gloria alone.""That would be very kind of you, Jimmy." Nick said. "There was no place for Marco in our setup. Here you are, still representing Detroit, and we don't need any help. We have a successful business, make good profits and are straight with the law."

"I know. I'm so glad it's turning out that way for Gloria, and you — that's what I intended all along."

"Since we're leveling with each other at last, I should let you know," Nick added, "that the local sheriff is on to you, and he has proof. Once he can put this together your prints from the hotel room with Chicago police and the FBI, they will have enough evidence to nail you for Charles Simmons's murder"

"I don't think so," Jimmy said with a grin, "Because I didn't do it."

"He's right, Nick," Gloria said. "You haven't talked about it with Patrick. He told me Candicci confessed to the Simmons murder.

"Not to mention that the feds are extremely interested in the old records found in that safe and could press charges," Nick said. "The Rockville County Sheriff sent his deputy to the hospital interview Patrick as a person of interest in Candicci's death. "

"Aw crap, here we go again," Jimmy said. "Maybe I can go talk to the sheriff."

"Not necessary, Nick said. "First of all, when he brought that up in Patrick's hospital room, Ross Hunter and his wife were visiting. They were Kitty's hosts when she first came to America. They took up his defense — he's a corporate attorney and so is she. He was delighted to do a little trial defense work and referred him to the FBI and the Chicago police, since they are already handling the case.

"As for the County Clerk, Tubby Balquier, who runs things in Rock County, I've already gone over all that with him. Tubby's up for reelection next fall and doesn't want to make any waves."

"Tubby, eh?" Jimmy chuckled. I guess I taught you how to get along with fat cats."

"Oh yeah. Chicago's even more political than Rockville. If you don't poke the bear in this county, nobody's gonna alert Chicago politicians to stir things up either. Do we have a deal?"

"I've told you in the past, I have no future but to keep the roughnecks from taking over the Detroit operation, trying to save my neck. You pay me back the funds you used for seed capital, and we're square. I'll hang on as long as I can, but I can't make any promises about what comes next."

"Fair enough. Maybe by then everybody will forget about it," Nick said.

"I guess I should just go quietly back to Detroit and only see you and Gloria at weddings, birthdays and family celebrations."

"Thanks, Jimmy." Gloria gave him a great big hug.

Chapter Forty-Two

Aweek later, when Patrick completed his tour of the construction site, he dropped by the farmhouse office to update Nick on project progress. Nick in turn filled him in on Romo's visit. He reported that Romo agreed to quit Chicago, leave McGurk and Gloria strictly alone and allow them to conduct their business as they saw fit. In return Nick promised he would never release any knowledge he had about any of Romo's crimes to the FBI or Chicago police. Romo had promised to cause no trouble for Gloria and Nick. So he could hold on to the gains made by Candicci and save his own skin, he accepted the deal.

"And he'll quit trying take over Joe's Chicago operations," Nick said.

"Isn't it ironic? Patrick said. "The County Clerk's corruption gave you the break you needed to do the right thing."

"When you look at the big picture, seems fair to me."

Patrick drove up the ramp to Interstate 90 on his way back to the office and joined the stream of traffic. The drone of news in the background switched to a clip from a right-wing candidate in a southern governor's race. "My opposing candidate's corrupt administration has flooded our border with criminals, rapists and drug addicts, who have increased the rate of violent crime throughout the country."

Lying to present the case for a candidate was nothing new, he thought, but today's politicians conformed to the new style — they concocted preposterous, implausible narratives, accusing others of the very misdeeds they themselves were committing.

Such thuggery was nearly identical to the business-as-usual that Joe Bohannon and Detroit's Jimmy Romo had conducted throughout their criminal careers. Locally Chicago Joe had offered society's misfits, minor criminals and outcasts membership in his welcoming crime family. He had maintained control over them through intimidation and fear of his retaliation for disobedience. Those who dared to defy him were soon denounced and discarded on the ash heap of the disloyal. Most of them — men under threat of ruined political careers — either maintained a mob-like omerta, disciplined silence, or persisting, would live to regret throwing away their future for such a futile, merit-less cause.

Thugs and politicians had much less success, Patrick noticed, when opposed by smart and determined women. They first tried to dismiss them as too fat, too ugly or too pushy to be physically attractive or simply "not my type." For the few women who had defied them either in court or had resisted blackmail, they took their cases to the court of public opinion, which generally accepted their version,

The analogy seemed apt, even as Patrick's thoughts returned to Gloria. While her mother Candy had won over Joe through her physical appeal, submission, and love over the years, Gloria had captivated him with her charm and intelligence. When deserted by Patrick she found a way to earn her own economic independence through her fortunate marriage and business partnership with her adoring mate Nick. Through her own intuition and skill, she had made peace with the mob and earned freedom from its influence.

Maybe Kitty was right. Those misguided men ought to step aside and let some woman take over. The right woman candidates might hold the keys to the survival of the democratic system.

Chapter Forty-Three

Together at last in their apartment home again, Kitty was bursting with questions she had wanted to ask Patrick while in captivity about her new life in America.

"When Candicci held me prisoner, he listen to that awful FIX News channel all day long. I'm still confused about how you do things in this country. Isn't this election year a little out of the ordinary?"

"Indeed, it is," Patrick said. "I've been watching this for months. Other than telling us how terrible their competition is and how they'll return America's its past greatness, these bossy bigots say they can run things better. But they have no proposals on how they would do itThese men have no policy, no plans, no vision for the future.

"They tell people the country is in decline and attack groups — immigrants, Blacks, Jews, Muslims, liberals — claiming that each group is responsible for some or other of the ills of this country, such as violent crime or anti-government activities. Anything to hold on to the vote of old white guys who feel threatened. Their aim is to divide us and make us forget the democratic principles of the founders we all hold in common, despite our differences."

"I can see that." Kitty said. "When one congressman says, when he accuses opponents of cheating and corruption — all of them decent and honorable men — it's a confession of his own guilt. He's like a cheating husband, who accuses his wife of his own misdeeds."

Patrick reddened at the thought. This would be the main challenge in his marriage — to stay on the straight and narrow and focus on his lovely bride. Kitty had made that easy, with her beauty, charm and intelligent companionship. He hoped he would never forget it.

"It's been going on for a long time," Patrick continued, "The mob does the same thing. They take in society's outcasts, make them part of 'the family,' and let them feel they belong. The better they serve the boss, the more perks, money, and authority they earn in the group. It has always worked for Detroit's Jimmy Romo, the big Chicago boss Sal Francone, and on down the line to the underbosses, like Joe Bohannon.

"The key to a mob boss's success," Patrick went on, "is to stay out of sight, be unpredictable and keep his underlings in fear. He makes them do the dirty work. He can change his mind at any minute and turn on anyone who displeases him or steps out of line. The punishment for his displeasure can be brutal, and in some cases, fatal."

"You'll have to admit, though, that Chicago Joe is a lot more fun than these brutes," Kitty said. "Did you ever notice that these bigots never smile? Joe doesn't take himself too seriously, and he praises you when you do something well. He wants the best for his daughter, and he loves music! A fellow like that can't be all bad."

"Joe's a good client, too. He accepts our suggestions for improving the design. And he pays his bills, on time! He's a good boss. He's fair with his people. He encourages them, rewards their success, and gives them a stake in good results. Unlike most mob bosses, he's patient with them. He shows them their mistakes and gives them a chance to improve"

"Look at what he's doing for Gloria and Nick, helping them set up a legitimate business. He's a real human being."

"That's where comparison stops," Patrick said. "

Kitty turned to face Patrick. "With all this going on, I sometimes wonder if I picked the wrong country."

"No, you picked the right one. The reason you may be uncomfortable is, it seems overwhelming when the choice of candidates is up to you. But it's not that difficult. Not everyone has to lobby Congress, or make great speeches. Together, you and millions of your fellow citizens can come out and vote, and find other ways to speak your mind.

"We've proven over the years that if the average people band together and speak up for a cause, they can change history. Little things can add up to big results. The people's voice and their votes count."

"I see what you mean," Kitty said. "Listen to your neighbors, respect what they say — whether you agree or not — and show them what we have in common."

"Exactly. While democracy is messy and inefficient, there's strength in numbers. We must elect representatives who carry forward our common purpose. It may take a while, but concerted action can eventually steer this ocean liner in a new direction toward our common goals."

"What you need is a smart woman to get the country back on track." Kitty said. "Look how Gloria has handled her father and Jimmy Romo. She keeps them happy, and they protect her from the mob. They respect her, while she and Nick proceed with their legitimate business. The right woman in the White House would know how to lead us to do the important things for people and forget the petty goals of a few greedy, power-hungry men."

She regretted spoiling Patrick's mood with dumb questions about politicians he considered stupid and wrong. She hoped they could resume their closeness and recall those things that had first drawn them together. Now she wondered how and if they could resume their intimacy.

He walked to the dark glass facing the lake. Kitty followed. In the fading twilight a tourist boat hugging the shoreline headed northward on an evening sightseeing cruise. "They have a small band and dancing on those boats," he said. "The skyline view is spectacular. You would love it"

"Let's do it soon."

Chapter Forty-Four

Kitty had begun cooking again. She served an Irish stew she had been preparing all day. She baked fresh bread, which she served warm with Irish butter. From a large bottle she poured out two mugs of bitter ale, put them on their dining table and invited Patrick to sit.

"Warm food for a chilly night," Patrick said.

They dined contentedly.

After dinner, in celebration of their reunion, Kitty served her father's special Irish coffee, made with Jameson's Irish whiskey. two lumps of sugar and a dollop of whipped cream.

"What's that necklace you're wearing?"

"This?" She lifted the pendant from inside her shirt collar.

"It's my little surprise. When Ann and I visited your project recently, I had a long talk with Kitty. We made peace. She said, as your true love, it really belongs to me."

As quickly as she had revealed this, she froze. A chill of unease crept up her spine. Patrick's eyes widened. For once he was at a loss for words. She was terrified he would not like this.

"Mom's diamond pendant! Why, how?"

"She passed it to me as her final blessing of our marriage. Do you approve?" Relieved but still anxious, she waited.

"Do I? It's the best! The two most important women in my life have accepted each other."

'Oh, Patrick!" Does that mean we can have Little Mike over to play with our daughter?"

"Hmm. He's my son. We'd better make sure they always have a chaperon."

"True, these MacKenna males can hardly be trusted. But I'm glad you're a protective father." She was giddy with relief. They were able to open up to each other again. Now no subject — not even Gloria — was off limits.

After dinner, they undressed and lay on the bed. Patrick kissed her ear and whispered into it. "I know what you like!"

He put his hand beside her spine and massaged the tense tendon there until it rippled freely between his fingers. Kitty squealed with delight as the tension of past weeks drained from her and she relaxed like a rag doll. Her eyes lit up and she flipped him over on his back, kissed the middle of his flat stomach, and blew a trumpet blast with her lips.

"Now that was silly!" he said.

They were back to their old goofy selves, with no holds barred.

Her inhibitions dissolved, and she laid her head on his chest, his heartbeat, strong and dependable, his breathing quick.

"Betcha can't catch me," she said, and hopped out of the bed toward the chair across the room. But Patrick rose and caught her with arms around her shoulders and pulled her to him. Their lips met in a crush, accidentally at first, then desperately. His mouth was soft yet eager, tentative, then firm, exploring. This quick reveal of his pent-up need exploded behind her shuttered eyes and slaked her urgent thirst. Months of longing poured from her devouring lips and yearning breast. He held her there, now a trembling leaf, gently pressing against his muscled chest for what seemed forever.

He bore her gently back into their marriage bed.

A night of joy and celebration followed. Sorrow fled.

Chapter Forty-Five

In their transports of pleasure, they had left the curtains open. Kitty awoke to a red and golden sunrise on the lake. Patrick was up, and the welcome aroma of breakfast drifted in the air.

Kitty showered and donned a frilly robe to greet Patrick.

"The sleeping beauty appears!" Patrick remarked from his post at the stove.

She gave Patrick a kiss on the cheek and sat. He poured coffee and set a plate with an omelet, bacon and a biscuit, before her.

"My goodness, you were full of surprises last night," he said, and sat down with her to eat.

"As you are this morning," she replied.

"Oh, I'm hardly finished with that," he said mysteriously.

"You know, I've been thinking about my new kitchen. In the Bond Street house, I said I could deal with the old one. When we find our new place, I want a good gas range, double ovens, a microwave — the works."

"Then you shall have them!" Patrick declared. "A fine cook requires adequate work space and the best of equipment."

"But how? We're done with the Victorian wreck. We don't have a place to live."

"Well, I have a slight modification to suggest in our plans."

"Really? What is it?"

"It's a surprise. First, let's enjoy our food while it's hot."

They savored the excellent breakfast. While she sipped her coffee, Kitty could no longer contain herself, "Now I'm dying to know about your surprise."

Patrick cleared the table and unrolled a set of plans. Boldface lettering on the cover sheet read:

New Residence For

Mr. And Mrs. Patrick Mackenna

39 Forest Creek Drive, St. Louis, Missouri

Centered on the page above the title was a perspective drawing, rendered in pencil, of a house set among trees with low sweeping lines. Wide, deep-set windows invited the inside out and the outside in. Generous roof overhangs, low brick walls and a covered walkway sheltered a flower-lined path leading from a detached garage to the side door.

"What if we moved in here instead?"

"We're really going?" Kitty's eyes lit up and began to fill with tears.

"If you want to go, I'll start work at Childress & Marks the first of next month. "I'll sign the contract to buy the lot tomorrow. Unless you'd rather not."

"Are you kidding?"

Kitty pulled him out of his chair and kissed him.

◊

On a Friday night the turmoil of another week was over. After a long day struggling with the final details of packing and shipping their possessions, Patrick and Kitty sat in the Cloistered Oyster for a late dinner.

"What do yov think Patrick? If there were no fire, would we have stayed?

"No way. Based on Chet's final inspection we'd already been released from the deal."

"But what about that beautiful architect's estate?" Kitty's look was questioning but desperate. "When the body was gone and the murder was solved, as you've often said, all that would remain were the normal problems any historic house of that age would have."

"Even so, Chet was right. He pointed out so many defects, we had to consider the other side of this. We needed a very expensive roof replacement. We had so many gables, parapets and valleys to waterproof, along with a very steep slope, the cost of restoration would have been astronomical. Then there were the structural repairs inside: a cracked foundation, removing all that coal from the basement and a new, very expensive heating system. New electrical wiring was needed throughout. On our last visit to the site, that grotesque mansion, with its curlicues and pretentious heights, crumbling toward collapse, looked ugly to me. Besides, it was totally unsuited to family life, beside a retired and desolate graveyard of Chicago's past industrial glory. It was devoid of the clean lines, organic materials, and closeness to nature both you and I admire. And even without Candicci, what about all the spooky stuff we couldn't explain?

"I thought the spirits would be friendly," Kitty said, "but those gangsters were the embodiment of evil. The property was doomed, and I was happy to give up. I do feel sorry for Hensley and Charlie, though, Their investment up in smoke."

"These deductions from our proposed purchase offer would have cut the price so much it would have killed the deal anyway.

"It was Charlie Simmons who really lost out."

"So sad. As to the house, this monster has been on the market so long, the fire sealed its doom. Wilson will need to use his insurance money to demolish the property. The land might be worth more than the building. After paying off the mortgage, he might break even on the deal."

"But we'll rescue our dream—at least my dream!" Kitty said.

"And mine as well. We'll have a great home for raising our family, and our architect's estate after all, even better than we'd hoped for. And I won't have to fight the mob when I'm designing projects."

"A fresh start. Maybe we can get it right this time!"

Chapter Forty-Six

On a perfect day in June, seven months apter the informal opening and testing of all systems, the resort was ready for prime time. The multistory Chicago Casino Hotel proudly overlooked the Rock River and marina. The other side faced the casino, restaurants, central pool and recreation patio. The lakeside chalets and the lake lay beyond. They were set on gentle hills, just as Patrick had envisioned them in his first color sketches. As he steered into the newly paved access drive of the resort, he recalled the chaos at the groundbreaking event. On that occasion Candicci's ragtag crew had parked cars, When the dedication ceremony was under way, a thunderstorm overtook the gathering, resulting in all kinds of bad outcomes. Tonight, uniformed attendants wearing peaked caps, the Andy Frain logo on their sleeves, and dark glasses against the late afternoon sun, guided visitors to overflow parking in surrounding fields. In the grassy hollow facing the teahouse island families barbecued, picnicked, and joined tours of the new hotel.

This was a small venue for the Corsairs — only five thousand were expected. Their big show was the next night at the United Center. With its glass walls retracted, the teahouse made a splendid bandstand. About

500 folding chairs had been set up for honored guests in rows right across the channel from the island structure. The rest of the crowd sat on blankets or their own portable chairs in the natural amphitheater facing the island stage.

Patrick and Kitty surveyed the scene from the concierge floor at the top of the hotel. Kitty's parents, visiting from Ireland, joined Sea,mus and Lily by the bassinet in the bedroom, where baby Erin slept peacefully. The grandparents were content to tend to their new grandbaby, overlook the concert below, and watch the special Corsairs Live event broadcast on MTV.

At five p.m. the hotel tours ended. Detective Sergeant O'Malley, who took this assignment out of his jurisdiction as a courtesy to the local sheriff, and FBI Special Agent Radwinski stood by the doors of the lobby. Their crew checked guest passes and hotel room keys at the entrance. Dignitaries gathered there for a buffet and cocktails in the main dining room of the hotel, along with Joe Bohannon, his wife Candy, his daughter Gloria, and Nick McGurk.

When Patrick and Kitty came down the elevator and joined Ellen and Chet greeted Patrick with a hearty embrace.

"Welcome, Nuezings!" Patrick said.

"Not bad for a first try, right?" Chet looked around in amazement at the crowds.

"Pretty darned close," Patrick replied. "Looks just the way we originally imagined it. The amphitheater was sort of an afterthought. But knowing Joe's musical interests, we couldn't disappoint him."

Joe Bohannon joined the two couples and introduced them to a slight, alert man with thinning gray hair and a dark grey business suit. "Folks, this is Isaac Gold, a friend of mine and long-time manager of the Corsairs." He greeted the four of them.

"Kitty and I have always loved your group's Paris Hotel. I thought about the song when I was over there."

"You'll hear that one tonight," Gold said. "The fans won't let them off the stage without it. They're warming up right now for the show, but they send their heartfelt greetings. Compliments you and your team on the fine architecture of this complex."

"The Mandicott family are especially pleased to have you here at this grand opening," Joe said, "and I'm over the moon."

"Much obliged, Joe," Gold said. "You ought to come and see us when you're in L.A."

"I'd love to when I go out west. Maybe in three years or so," Joe said. "But it won't be theasible by then unless I get out early for good behavior."

"Get out?" Gold said.

"I cut a five-year deal with the feds. Due to our plea negotiation, at least it includes release from all charges at the end and will be served at the nice, new federal residential facility north of Phoenix.

"Don't forget this was not for any of our Chicago operations, or this project," Joe reminded him. "You remember, I had another career, before the music business? I also was in sports, signing up high school athletic stars for professional teams, when we ran amok of a new federal law barring those deals with young athletes. You may recall that I was comprehended as a an auspicious person at that time."

"Yeah. Damned shame." Gold was long accustomed to Joe's manner sof speech.

"Now, don't worry about me. That collectional center, if you can even call it that, is a country club is like a country club, showplace of the whole system."

"You put the feds off for ten years, anyway," Gold said. "Look at all you've accomplished in the meantime — a proud legacy for your daughter."

At seven, barbecue fires were quenched, crowds filed into the amphitheater, and picnickers sat on their blankets on the grass. Patrick, Kitty, Chet and Ellen sat on their own camp chairs in the hollow facing the island. Their attention focused on the teahouse, transformed into a stylish stage by sweeping aside the glass walls. In front of them the invited dignitaries and special guests filed into their reserved folding chairs. Technicians ran sound checks of the complex array of amplifiers and speakers mounted on the building and transmitted to remote speaker towers located at the fringe of the woods bordering the audience.

The sun hung low in the west, cast its last rays on the blanket sitters in the hollow and slid slowly behind the sylvan foliage beyond the lake, glimmering on the rippling water and imparting a pink glow to a cloudless sky. They waited in hushed expectancy, the still air bracing for the coming explosion of sound.

With a stirring sequence of chords, lights flooded the island and illuminated the Corsairs, seven of them in all, arrayed in bearded, scruffy splendor across the stage. They opened with their classic tune about gambling at cards. The music reminded Patrick of his journey to this point in his life. and concluded he'd begun winning his hands.

When they played "Rise and Fall," he reflected on how it feels when your dreams come true and it's not quite like you planned. When they picked up the tempo with "Breakneck Speed," Patrick was glad at last he'd been able to slow down.

When he heard the tinkling guitars of the intro to "Paris Hotel," he put an arm around Kitty and hugged her. As the lyrics suggested, their separate visits to the City of Light had been about searching for themselves in a new and different place. The guitar duel between the two lead players made him laugh — it reminded him of his literal French translation of English expressions versus the correct idiomatic responses so perfectly articulated and pronounced by the French. Here now at the Chicago Casino and Hotel, he looked around him at all they had accomplished in their dream project.

The song lyrics reminded him of Kitty's miraculous venture from the Old World. She had packed her hopes and dreams to take her chances on the new. Patrick's hopes were pinned on giving her story a happy ending. As the lights came up again for a rousing encore, he looked forward to tomorrow morning, when they would get on that highway and take it to the limit one more time. The lights dimmed for the last time to thunderous applause.

The four of them sat in the moonlight as the few remaining spectators gathered picnic baskets, folding chairs and blankets and filed back to their cars.

The power went down, leaving only battery-operated work lights. His eyes adjusted to the dim moonlight as they watched the crew strike the set. As always after any show, he felt sad to see the magic undone, unwilling to break the spell. A swarm of roadies dismantled light towers, packed away electronic amplifiers, speakers, coiled miles of cable and the instruments — guitars, electric pianos, drum sets and horns. They rolled the cases across the bridge and loaded them into a fleet of semi-trailers waiting on the creek's opposite shore. At last Patrick and Kitty were left alone with Ellen and Chet in the empty glen.

The four of them watched the last spectators leave, but remained seated, unwilling to break the spell.

"I don't ever want this to end," Patrick said.

"Not just the concert." Kitty looked into his eyes. "I don't want us to end."

"Now we can settle down," Patrick said.

"With your nose for trouble, I hope you can," Kitty said.

"You know I can't help it., and I love you more than any old project."

"Don't worry Patrick, I took you for better or worse. I left a boring life in Ireland because I wanted it to be exciting."

"That, at least, I can guarantee." Patrick kissed her tenderly, and the four walked back to the hotel in the moonlight. Patrick and Kitty rejoined their family in the hotel. Ellen and Chet left to get home to the kids.

Chet mused on the way home. He had tried to discourage Patrick from gambling on long shots. He'd first resisted and later urged him to trust Chicago Joe. But what would happen when Gloria and Nick took over? Despite Nick's previous mob association and his struggle to free himself from the Detroit organization, could he succeed?

Patrick urged Chet to dream when he didn't dare. Bold and blind to danger, he took the risks for both of them. Afterward Chet would suffer and die in silence and struggle, head down, to fix all the trouble Patrick faced. True, as Ellen liked to point out, he wasn't Patrick's keeper. But still he had long been his protector, mentor and inspiration to carry on.

Holdroyd & Robb was entering a new generation, with the younger leaders, including Patrick, if he had stayed, admitted to the firm as principals. After completion of the casino resort, clients would become more conventional, Patrick predicted, and gangster involvement with the firm would fade away.

Chet hoped he was right.

Chapter Forty-Seven

With the casino and hotel buildings finished and the first concert behind them, Chet was free to focus on technical details. He designed adjustments to the teahouse stage, site improvements, and other new buildings in the complex. His location moved from his cubicle to the office next to Jason Holdroyd, with Chet Neuzing, Executive Vice President, painted on the old-fashioned, pebbled glass door. For the present, Patrick's corner office of the Chief Architect would remain empty, a daily reminder of Chet's grief at losing his vital presence.

Chet wished him and his new bride all the success and happiness they deserved. He felt sure Patrick would find many others, at least as able as he, eager to help and support him. Chet would miss him terribly, but he couldn't leave what he had here — a career, a growing family and a deep love for this wicked old city. Besides, he was a die-hard Cubs fan.

As a witness to this period in the life of Patrick MacKenna, Chet had also lived it, as his best friend and confidant. Late at night over the phone, in the office and at their many meals and after-work sessions together at the Cloistered Oyster bar, they were extensions of each other's thoughts and actions. He would sorely miss him. But he and his wife Ellen were settled in life, with kids in school, an apartment building they owned and managed, and many local and professional obligations to honor.

Mike MacKenna, as usual, continued his leading role in Patrick's life — staking out new markets and future building projects. He'd lately told Patrick he had a queasy feeling about Chicago. While it would continue to grow and expand beyond all reasonable expectations, the State of Illinois was slowly strangling itself and saddling future citizens with debt. Decades of corrupt government were taking their toll. Of course, its many creative citizens would help it rise again from the ashes.

As Patrick moved on, however, so did the Outfit. Even the mob leaders sensed a coming reform and change of climate. One capo, Solly Abrams, moved his Chicago operations to Southwestern Illinois, which included the Metro East area opposite St. Louis. There he could operate without direct supervision of the Chicago bosses and take advantage of the wealth in his new surroundings. Solly came up in the traditional rackets. Riverside gambling casinos, now legalized in both Illinois and Missouri, were his latest prime candidates.

In St. Louis Mike met the new mayor, served on the Visitor and Convention Bureau, and volunteered for the City-Arch-River Board, planning and raising raise money for the St. Louis 250th anniversary celebration in 2014.

Mike gave his local business to the old-line architectural and engineering firm, Childress & Marks. He helped them expand their job portfolio from bridges, highways and wastewater collection and treatment systems, and added industrial, commercial and government building design. He cultivated the friendship of a hotel developer who planned to take over a ten-story cotton exchange warehouse right next to downtown and adjacent to the new St. Louis Blues hockey arena. Mike introduced the hotel developer to Patrick MacKenna, who employed his new staff to implement his innovative idea: to carve a new light well and courtyard right in the middle of the large warehouse floor plan. This allowed light and air into the center of this massive building. They completed their design with a hotel lobby, meeting rooms and restaurants at ground level, parking spaces on two levels above that, a floor of workout facilities, a swimming pool, and several floors of hotel rooms above.

Nick and Gloria McGurk were not only family. They also became celebrity hosts. She loved to appear in the casino, giving lessons to new gamblers and dancing to the rhythms of tribute bands to the big names of the 40s and 50s — The Glenn Miller Orchestra, Harry James, Tommy Dorsey, Frank Sinatra imitator Michael Bublé, and jazz combos reminiscent of Dave Brubeck. They entertained in the nightclub, on the man-made island in the lake accessed by a covered bridge.

"You did pretty well, despite the mob," Kitty told him. "But, better yet, you cracked the biggest case of all. You solved the puzzle of what's best for the MacKenna family!"

Patrick undertook Mike MacKenna's latest projects at the St. Louis firm of Childress & Marks and was soon made a principal of the historic company. He was building the dream house they really wanted in half the time he expended trying to figure out how to restore the Victorian wreck.

He had abandoned the hustle in "the city of big shoulders," and the city motto, "I Will." He traded it for the St. Louis area's four hundred municipal government units, whose fractious local politicians flaunted an unspoken attitude, "I Won't." He slowed down to the pace and friendly yet surprisingly cosmopolitan atmosphere of the Gateway City, which many locals called a "big small-town." He scarcely missed the furious, insistent pace of the larger metropolis. Kitty concluded it would be the perfect place to bring up children in their new family.

Before he left Patri,ck told Chet, his colleague and best friend, he had scored about even, with as many wins as losses. But the glass, which he once thought half-empty, now looked half full. Now he cared. He had a wife and a family to love, support — and protect. Maybe he could try to improve his new city, be a force for good.

Could he get a second chance? He would never know if he didn't try.

Acknowledgments

This book would not have been possible without the help, support and encouragement of my friends and colleagues in St. Louis Writers Guild, including Brad R. Cook, Jessica Mathews, Cherie Postill, Larry Duerbeck, David Margolis, Ed Protzel, Joe Hauser, and many others too numerous to name.

I am especially appreciative of the encouragement I got from Bonnie Jo Campbell, and the evaluation, critiques, and edits I received from her very smart friends, who made numerous suggestions to help me bring this work to its fullest potential.

While many have helped to improve this book, all errors are mine.

—Peter H. Green, St. Louis, July, 2025

About the Author

Peter as Godfather

PETER H. GREEN, a writer, architect and city planner, found his father's 400 World War II letters and humorous war stories, his mother's writings and his family's funny doings too good a tale to keep to himself, so he launched a second career as a writer.

When the pandemic came along, Peter tackled a project he was afraid to put off any longer. While he still had his faculties, could remember his life and could sit up and take nourishment, he wrote his illustrated memoir, Becoming an Architect: My Voyage of Discovery.

Peter has written biographical memoirs of his World War II-era family and three architectural mysteries featuring architect-amateur sleuth, Patrick MacKenna. He lives in St. Louis with his wife Connie, has "two married daughters and three very young grandchildren. A complete list of his works, purchase links and story of the last pet he owned, "The Night We Ruined the Dog," his website: www.AuthorPeterGreen.com.

Go to website

Before you go …

Writers depend on readers to get out the word about theirwork.

What you think matters!

Please take a minute to to put a comment on the Reviews page for this book on your favorite bookstore site, social network or Goodreads. com. Some frequently visited book sites appear on my bookstore page:

https://authorpetergreen.com/petes-books/ at the QR Code below;

Go to Pete's Books

www.ingramcontent.com/pod-product-compliance
Lightning Source LLC
Chambersburg PA
CBHW071254190726
48292CB00007B/2529